Praise for Emery Sanborne's *Modus Vivendi*

Blue Ribbon Rating: 4.5 "...a very sexy and passionate romance involving two men and a woman that find their love and friendship threatened by society's expectations. The powerful emotions conveyed throughout the story drew me in and made me feel a part of the story. MODUS VIVENDI is a wonderful tale of love that is sure to appeal to many."

~ *Anita, Romance Junkies Reviews*

Modus Vivendi

Emery Sanborne

A Samhain Publishing, Ltd. publication.

Samhain Publishing, Ltd.
577 Mulberry Street, Suite 1520
Macon, GA 31201
www.samhainpublishing.com

Modus Vivendi
Copyright © 2008 by Emery Sanborne
Print ISBN: 978-1-59998-821-4
Digital ISBN: 1-59998-604-3

Editing by Anne Scott
Cover by Dawn Seewer

First Samhain Publishing, Ltd. electronic publication: September 2007
First Samhain Publishing, Ltd. print publication: July 2008

Dedication

To Philippa Grey-Gerou for keeping me grounded and lending a ready ear. I couldn't ask for a better friend.

To Mr. K., my seventh grade English teacher, who introduced me to the joys of writing.

To Mom.

Chapter One

It amazed Drea Samuels how quickly things fell apart. Twelve years of friendship didn't seem to add up to much, especially with a war on. Without so much as a by-your-leave, her friends had gone and signed up to fight the Kaiser in the summer of 1917. That they'd gone behind her back wasn't half as bad as the fact that they waited until barely a week before shipping out to tell her. Never in her nineteen years had she felt so betrayed.

To hell with them. If Aidan Morrison and Virgil Craig wanted to be stupid and risk getting killed in a war they had no business fighting, fine. It was their idiot decision; they had to live with it.

She hadn't seen either of them in the four days following the news of their enlistment. It was a reasonable cooling-off period. Usually, they gave her a week to get over her anger and come to them. She didn't have that luxury now.

Aidan showed up on her porch Wednesday midafternoon while she was busy shelling peas for dinner. If she weren't still so damned angry at him, Drea might have realized something was amiss much sooner.

"Hey, Drea." He leaned on the newel support post, his normally unguarded gaze never once directly meeting hers.

"Aidan," she replied coolly. If he had been Virgil, she would have ignored him altogether. But he was Aidan, and she could never bring herself to be as mean to him as to Virgil.

Shifting his feet, he said, "Fine afternoon, isn't it?"

"Fine week. As a matter of fact, it's the perfect weather to get thrown over by one's friends." All right, so maybe a little mean.

He did look at her then, brown eyes soulful. "God, Drea, you don't know how sorry I am about this. We never meant to hurt you."

"Did you honestly think I'd be happy for you? I want friends, not fool boys who think playing hero is going to make them into men!" She set the bowl of peas aside before standing up. She was angry enough without having to clean peas off the porch. "Jesus Christ, Aidan, do either of you know me at all?"

Aidan looked off into the distance. "That's why we waited to tell you for as long as we did."

"Wait to tell me so there wouldn't be a damned thing I could do to stop you?"

"Pretty much," he admitted quietly.

If she thought it would do any good, she would have hit him.

"Obviously you haven't changed your mind," she spat, long arms crossed over her unremarkable chest. Less a gesture of defensiveness than one of holding herself in check, physically if not verbally. "So, why are you here?"

"I wanted to talk. Knew better, but had to try anyway." Closing his eyes, he leaned his head back against the post and sighed.

"Well, I don't have all day. If you're going to talk, talk and be done with it."

One eye peeked open and fixed on her. "I would if someone would shut up long enough," Aidan said, a hint of amusement in his voice. "If I didn't love you so much, girl, I probably would have killed you long before now."

Drea fought the smile tugging at her lips. He always found a way to get past her anger. Blowing a few stray coppery strands of hair out of her face in frustration, she sighed. "I really hate you sometimes, you know that?" But the words lacked any real heat.

"I've gotten that impression from time to time." He grinned.

She sat down again. When she spoke, the edge was gone from her voice. "Don't think I'm not still mad at you. But you can say your piece without me biting your head off."

Aidan shoved his hands in his pockets and faced her. He hesitated before plunging ahead. "I've got something I want you to consider while I'm gone."

Lead settled in Drea's stomach. She hoped this wasn't heading where it seemed to be. She opened her mouth, but Aidan held up his hand to stay her protest.

"Please, don't say anything," he pleaded. "I know I'm not going about this the right way, but I need to get it off my chest before I leave. There's no telling if I'll be coming back, and I'd rather not have any regrets if I can help it." He paused, removing his right hand from his pants pocket as he stepped forward to set an object on the table.

That same heavy feeling in her gut told her she didn't need to look to know what he had set down. But she looked anyway. Before her lay a silver ring composed of three strands interwoven to form a continuous loop.

"I don't want an answer either way. I wanted you to know that you're one of the two most important people in my life, Drea, and seeing as I can't rightly ask Virgil... All I'm asking is

9

that you think about it. Something to consider. That's it, no more, no less."

Aidan was long gone before Drea found her voice again.

Picking up the ring, she studied it closely. "Aidan, you idiot, why'd you have to go and ruin everything?"

℘

Drea cut through the field between her house and Virgil's. The boys were due to ship out the next day, and she had yet to see or hear from Virgil, which left her no choice but to make sure he heard from her. She'd expected him to come to her, especially after the stunt Aidan pulled. Maybe Virgil didn't know. Or did he know and was pissed at them both? No, he would have shown up on her doorstep in high dudgeon, possibly dragging Aidan in tow and wanting to know what in the hell they were thinking.

She cursed Aidan again as she opened the door to the Craigs' carriage house. As expected, she found Virgil busy tinkering with his motorcycle. Whenever he had time to spare, he could be found either riding the bike or trying to make it run better. The bike had been a gift from his uncle on his sixteenth birthday, along with his first trip to Madam Violet's brothel in Grand Rapids to mark the occasion of finally becoming man.

Virgil looked up as the door shut, strands of dark hair falling loosely over his eyes. Brushing it back, he grinned, gray eyes dancing. "Figured you'd come by eventually."

"The road goes both ways, you know," she said tartly.

"How long have we known each other, Drea? Give me some credit." Attention back on the bike, he switched one wrench for another. He continued speaking, tone mirthful. "One too many tongue lashings and well-aimed punches have taught me well. Knew it was a bad idea when we taught you how to fight. It's always best to let you cool off and come to me."

"You're the damned pot calling the kettle black."

He set the wrench down, wiped his hands and stood, turning to face Drea. "I never said I wasn't guilty of the same. And being that I am of admittedly similar temperament, if I can't judge you, who can?"

She couldn't argue with that. And so far, things seemed normal. No awkwardness or anger. He didn't know. And he wouldn't ever know, if she could help it. She'd let Aidan have his peace of mind and, when he got back, she'd give him the ring and it would all go away. Until then, she would wear it around her neck to keep an eye on it. It wouldn't do to lose the ring, would it?

"Drea, you fall asleep on me?" Virgil came to stand next to her.

"Huh? No, just thinking," she replied. "So you're really going through with the enlistment?"

"Yeah, we are." He frowned. "Aidan's dead set on going, and I can't let him go alone."

"No, I guess you can't," she sighed. "Don't know what I'm going to do around here with both of you gone."

"You'll figure something out. I wouldn't be surprised if you discovered we've been holding you back all these years."

"From what? This is Morton's Pointe, not Detroit or even Grand Rapids. You get this far north in Michigan and about the only excitement you can look forward to is the yearly influx of summer tourists from those cities."

"You'll figure it out," he said with conviction. "There are plenty of opportunities here if you know where to look."

"Well, the one opportunity I want, Daddy's against letting me have. I've helped him out in that store since I was old enough to see over the counter, yet he refuses to let me take on more responsibilities." She grinned. "I suppose I could go work for your uncle in your place this fall."

Virgil glared. "Don't even joke about that."

"What, because I'm a woman and have no place in business?"

"No, because you know as well as I do what an insufferable, pigheaded asshole Uncle Raymond is." Smirking, he added, "*And* you're a woman who has no place in business. He's worse than your daddy that way."

"Your uncle's had a few good moments."

"Few and far between..." His words trailed off as his gaze fixed on her neck and traveled down.

Her hand immediately went to the chain, trying to tuck it away. It must have slipped out on the walk over.

But Virgil grabbed it and raised the ring to get a better look. "What are you doing with Great-Gran Morrison's ring?" he asked, his voice too controlled, the way it got right before he exploded.

"Nothing, I, um..." She couldn't think of a plausible excuse. Virgil *would* recognize it. She had, too, once she got over the shock of what Aidan had done. It had been Aidan's second most treasured possession for as long as they knew him, next to a battered copy of Shakespeare. He'd inherited it from his great-gran "to give to a special someone someday".

Virgil tugged hard enough that the metal dug into her neck.

"You're going to break the chain!" She tried unsuccessfully to free it from his grasp.

He dropped the ring with disgust. "I'm going to kill him."

"No, you're not. And he never actually asked." Drea tucked the ring under her shirt, rubbing her neck where the chain had cut into it.

"And you probably didn't *actually* reply," he said bitterly. "But he gave the ring to you, and you're wearing it."

Drea's temper, which had been on constant simmer since this whole mess began, finally exploded through the shock of it all. "It's not as if I wanted him to!"

"I am going to kill him," Virgil growled. "He had no right do to that to us."

"To me, you mean."

"No, to all of us. He went and fucked everything up." His fist slammed into the stable wall, sending dust down from the rafters.

Even the first time she had seen such a display of Virgil's temper, she hadn't been surprised. Probably because she had indulged in such displays of temper too many occasions to count. Drea knew that if she didn't hit or throw some inanimate object, she'd likely take it out on anyone around her.

Virgil turned on her, his gray eyes smoldering, strands of dark hair falling unheeded into his face. He was as pissed at her as he was at Aidan.

And he had no right to be.

"Don't you dare blame me for this. You're the ones running off to war, not me."

"If you don't want the ring, why haven't you given it back?"

"He didn't give me a chance to."

"You'd have found a way if you wanted to."

Drea felt her blood rise. She could hit Virgil and scream at him, but it wouldn't make a difference. Much as she hated the idea, she had to walk away. Before either of them did or said something they would regret.

She brushed past Virgil, intending on a stormy, door-slamming exit, but he pulled her back with a viselike grip on her upper arm.

"You are *not* walking away from this," he snarled.

She looked at him, looked at the hand restraining her, and at him again. She snorted derisively. "Yes, I am. And you know full well I'll make you regret it if you don't let me go right now."

A tense silence settled, stretching taut between them as they stood there immobile. Virgil moved first, pulling Drea against his chest, his mouth crushing down over hers. Surprise opened her mouth, allowing his tongue to gain entrance and claim her. It overwhelmed her and made her weak in a way that was far from unpleasant. She'd been kissed before, by Virgil, by Aidan and a few forgettable others. But not like this. Never this all-consuming, ache-inducing kind that drove all thought but one from her head. *More.*

When he pulled back, out of breath, Drea reacted on instinct. She slapped him. Hard enough to make her palm sting and the force of the blow reverberate up her arm.

"You goddamned bastard! How could—what in the hell, Virgil?" she shrieked.

He watched her darkly but didn't say a word.

"Virgil. What were you thinking?"

Still nothing. Maybe hitting him again would get a response. Before she could put thought into action, he grabbed her wrist and twisted it behind her, pulling her tight against him. He kissed her again, swallowing her protest. This kiss was more intense. She found herself responding. The desire for more had taken hold again, and she wasn't going to wait for him to give it to her. She kissed him back, hungry, demanding and pouring out every bit of anger she could no longer give voice to.

Virgil groaned, the sound so deep and low it rumbled through her. The hand that pinned her wrist abandoned it, grazing down her back, along her waist and farther downward, coming to rest on her bottom. His fingers dug into the soft flesh through her skirts, pulling her closer. Her breath caught sharply at the sudden awareness of his cock nudging hard and insistent through all their layers against her stomach. She really did that to him?

He pressed her against the carriage house wall, his lips working along her jawline toward her ear.

"God, Drea," he breathed, his voice husky. "You have no idea how many times I've imagined this, how many times I've almost done this when we've fought. Why do you think I'm the first one to walk away, more often than not?"

"This, Virgil?" she managed to speak with difficulty. His hands roamed over her body, eliciting feelings she'd had no idea of. When one wandered over her breast, squeezing, she cried out from a mixture of pain and pleasure. He did it again as his teeth came together on the tender skin of her neck. The sensation was electric. "Oh," she gasped.

Virgil gave a rich, deep chuckle that vibrated against her throat. "I should have known you'd be vocal."

"And what is that supposed to mean?" She attempted to sound indignant, but a breathless quality to her voice undermined any sternness. The buttons on the top of her dress gave way as Virgil slowly unfastened it, distracting her from a second attempt. "What are you—"

She got her answer in short order as his left hand found its way back to her breast, the thin cotton chemise doing little to block the heat and sensation against her sensitive skin. When Virgil slipped under the material, rough calluses of his palm caressing her, Drea was very glad to have the figure she did

15

that made it pointless to wear a corset. No amount of boning, metal, cloth or string had been able to shape her shapeless waist or make up for her small chest. And it made one less layer to contend with now.

Virgil started kissing her again. While his left hand toyed with her breast, his right journeyed down, grabbing at her skirt and slowly working it up. Soon, only her cotton bloomers lay between her and Virgil's denim. He abandoned her breast as both of his hands moved to untie the drawstring, leaving her drawers to pool at her feet.

It wasn't like she hadn't been naked around Virgil before. Or Aidan, for that matter. Until a few summers ago, the three of them had always gone skinny-dipping together in Lake Charlevoix, the local inland lake. It had two big advantages over nearby Lake Michigan—too rustic for the rich city tourists and a lot less bone-chilling cold. She knew swimming naked with the boys wasn't proper, but why get good clothes wet when no one could really see anything once you jumped in, anyway? Besides, it was Virgil and Aidan. Then the year she was fifteen, near the end of the summer, she'd turned around in time to find Virgil watching her hungrily. When she blinked, the look had vanished. She'd tried to act like nothing had happened, except Aidan hadn't met her eyes for the rest of the afternoon. On that day she realized that her boys were becoming men, and their relationship was likely to get complicated soon.

Complicated had finally arrived. First Aidan's "something to think about" and now this with Virgil. What had—

Drea's mind went completely blank as Virgil's hand ventured where even her own had only strayed once out of curiosity following the story he had told of his first trip to Madam Violet's brothel down in Grand Rapids with his uncle. But this wasn't like her own mortified forays, this was...tingly.

She could barely find her breath as Virgil drew back far enough to look at her while his finger kept circling over something hidden down there that made her knees turn to jelly. He pressed harder, and her body quivered in response.

"Like that?" He had that cocky grin he got when he knew he was right. She hated that grin. But she couldn't quite manage to tell him so. It took everything she had to keep upright.

Then he left off, his hand moving farther between her legs until a finger slipped up inside her.

For that she found her voice. "Virgil, what the hell are you doing?" It barely came out a whisper.

"Relax, Drea." His voice had a touch of tenderness. "Feel."

Feeling was about all she could do. Their current situation was very strange, but not in a bad way. It just wasn't like anything she had experienced before. Then, suddenly, it stopped being strange and kind of hurt, because he put two fingers where one seemed to fit fine.

She must have cried out, since Virgil's lips were suddenly against her ear, crooning softly, "It'll hurt maybe a minute, then it will be fine again."

The bastard turned out to be right. It went from hurting back to strange and then kind of good feeling. It didn't feel half as good as what he had first done, but she didn't mind it much, either.

His hand was gone and he was gone, not far, but enough for the air to be cold on her skin. Dazedly, she watched him unfasten and push down his pants, his cock springing free, stiff and deep red. It might have shocked her had she not caught him behind the barn the spring he turned fourteen. It had looked a lot like this then, except most of it had been hidden in his hand. All of that was supposed to fit inside her? No wonder women spoke of wedding nights with almost hushed fear.

Drea tried to back into the wall as he stepped forward. She wasn't scared. Drea Samuels didn't get scared. However, she was a touch overwhelmed at the moment.

"Drea, it'll be all right," he said gently, his hand coming up to brush a few stray strands of hair from her face. "I promise."

She swallowed. Virgil didn't make promises lightly. They were rare enough to mean something. So if he said it'd be all right, well, she'd believe him. She nodded, giving her assent.

He kissed her as he moved between her legs, the head of his cock nudging at the opening concealed there.

"It's gonna hurt like a son of a bitch at first," he warned her. "But it'll get better."

The protest died on her lips as he pressed inside. It did hurt, quick, sharp burning. The pain soon passed, replaced by a dull, fading ache and fullness. Not so bad. And definitely didn't hurt like a son of a bitch, except that first part.

"Drea?" he asked, a faint note of concern in his voice.

"If that's your idea of awful pain, Virgil Craig, you better be damned glad you aren't a woman. You'd never make it through a month," she teased, surprising herself.

Cracking a wry grin, he said, "It's what Madam Violet told me."

"Yeah, well, I think she was having you on."

It should seem odd, bantering like this, considering their current situation, with him buried inside her, yet it felt right. And that thought scared her. That kind of thinking meant trouble. Of course, if she'd meant to avoid trouble, she wouldn't be here now.

He pressed her into the wall, hands wrapping around the backs of her thighs and lifting her up, changing the position

18

enough so that he moved slightly inside her. Drea's mouth formed a silent "o" of surprise. Well, that was...interesting.

"Can you, maybe, do that again?" she asked uncertainly as she linked her ankles together behind him.

"That and more," he replied before capturing her mouth in a savoring kiss.

Everything was slow at first. The kiss, the gradual withdrawal and eventual return of his cock. Steady, easy, the pace and sensations built by degrees. As Drea lost herself in the rhythm, her body seeming to know how to move in response to Virgil, she began to feel really good. There definitely wasn't any more pain. And when one of his hands worked between them, finding that place he'd near worried her to distraction with earlier, she thought she might lose her mind. The world, her thoughts, it all narrowed down to sensation. A warm tension built deep inside, growing until she didn't think she could take anymore and then it released, and she fell over the edge into tingling nothingness. She had a vague awareness of Virgil going still and then crying out as he came inside her, filling her even more.

Silence descended, stillness, and Drea felt herself floating along in a contented oblivion. But it didn't last. Her worries came rushing back. The war and the boys leaving tomorrow, Aidan and the ring, this now with Virgil. Too much in too short a time. She had never felt more miserable in her life. The kind of misery that was pain, and this pain did hurt like a son of a bitch. She would have sold her soul for it to be a week ago, before any of this had happened.

Chapter Two

Redressing hurriedly, Drea left without a word or backward glance, as if she couldn't get away from him fast enough. And Virgil stood there, watching her run, pulling up his pants and refastening them automatically. Not since he'd boarded the train to come to Morton's Pointe to live with his uncle following his parents' deaths had he ever felt more lost.

Their friendship falling apart was inevitable, if he cared to think about it, and not one of them could carry the sole blame. Though Virgil would lay a good portion of it on Aidan's doorstep for starting the whole chain of events into motion with the war and...

Sighing, Virgil ran a hand roughly through his hair. "No, my man, you know good and well it was all going to hell before Aidan took a fancy to being a soldier."

The inevitable had started October two years earlier. He couldn't blame himself any more than he could blame Drea for pissing him off or Aidan for doing what he did. But it was very possible he could blame Bill Wellington. If Bill hadn't asked Drea to the Harvest Festival shindig, then Virgil never would have went off on Drea in a fit of jealous rage, even if he hadn't recognized it as jealousy at the time. And Aidan, who had been every bit as hurt by Drea's acceptance of Bill, had put aside his own feelings to play peacemaker between them yet again.

CB

"It ain't right, Drea. You're not going with him, end of discussion," Virgil bellowed.

Her face, flushed with fury, made her normally brilliant red hair dull in comparison. "You're not my goddamned father, Virgil. Bill asked. I'm going. End of discussion," she threw his words back at him.

"So we're not good enough for you suddenly?"

"Excuse me?"

"For the past nine years we've always gone to the festival, you, me and Aidan. *Every* year. It's what we do."

"Well, this year I thought I'd try something different," she said haughtily.

Virgil looked to Aidan for help. But Aidan shook his head.

"I'm not saying I care much for it either," he prefaced, "but it's not like we actually had set plans. We just happen to go together every year."

"But Bill Wellington?" Virgil whirled back on Drea. "Bill fucking Wellington? Bill, who we used to make fun of for being so portly we called him 'Beef Wellington'? Or have you forgotten that, too?"

Drea's fists clenched, and she raised her right one briefly before dropping it again. "Much as I'd love to hit you, I don't fancy having a sore hand for the festival." And with that, she'd turned on her heel and stormed out of the Morrison family barn, calling behind her, "I'm going, Virgil, and there ain't a damned thing you can do to stop me."

He'd show her there was a damned thing he could do about it! But Aidan held him back, his hand a solid grounding force on Virgil's shoulder. "You know you'll only make it worse if you keep on at her."

Virgil shrugged him off. "I don't know why you can't ever take my side."

"I didn't take her side, Virgil," Aidan said exasperated. "I never take sides, if I can help it."

"Bullshit." Virgil faced his friend. "You took her side just now."

"I said we didn't have plans, only pointed out the facts as they were. If it happened to be in her favor, well, that's the way of it." With a grimace, Aidan added, "Not that I'm thrilled to see her going with anyone, especially Bill. But the fact is, she's a free agent. We have no claims on her but what friendship has."

"No claims but what—" Virgil couldn't even finish. He let out a disgusted sigh that sounded close to a growl. "I don't get you sometimes, Aidan. You say you aren't thrilled, but you're standing there cool as a cucumber. Just once I'd like to see you get riled."

Aidan remained as collected as ever. "You and Drea get riled enough for me. Christ, if I got in on it, not one of us would be left standing."

He had a point. But Virgil wasn't in the mood to see reason. Drea had gone off and left him all worked up. And you couldn't fight with Aidan. But he was the only one around.

"Fuck it." He launched his right fist at Aidan's face.

Aidan barely managed to duck out of the way. "What in the hell did I do?"

"Not a goddamned thing." Virgil looked for another opening.

"Nothing is always a great reason for trying to take your best friend's head off," Aidan shouted. "Take it out on the barn door if you have to, but not me. I deserve better."

Aidan did deserve better. But that didn't matter to Virgil right now. "The barn door don't hit back." He swung again.

Aidan blocked him with reflexes born from being the youngest of five brothers. "If you're going to fight me, Virgil, you should be pissed at *me*. Not Drea, not Bill."

Virgil expected Aidan to back off, to try and talk him down some more or maybe walk away. What he never would have expected in a million years was for Aidan to grab a hold of his shirt, haul him forward and kiss him direct on the mouth. Aidan held him there, pulling him closer until the kiss stopped being a meeting of lips and became active and consuming. Virgil's mouth gave way in shock as Aidan deepened the kiss, tongue plunging in, punishing, claiming. There was anger in it and hunger and Virgil found himself responding in kind before he could even process what was going on. Virgil suddenly stumbled backward as Aidan pushed him away.

"There, now you can try and hit me." Aidan, surprisingly calm, stood braced to fight.

Virgil found breathing extremely difficult and thought next to impossible. Aidan's words barely registered as Virgil tried to wrap his head around what had happened. Aidan had kissed him. Aidan had fucking kissed him and—Virgil couldn't get it to make any sense. Especially with his cock straining against his jeans. "What in the hell did you do to me?" he asked, the question weighted with shock and a touch of fear.

"You wanted to fight me. Now you have an excuse to."

Aidan was lying. It wasn't in his nature to up and do something solely as an excuse to fight.

"That's not why you did it," Virgil called him on it.

Aidan's eyes widened in surprise. "Of course it is." Now even a blind man could see that he lied. "Fucking hit me already, would you, Virgil." It wasn't a command so much as a

23

plea. "Please."

He couldn't just stand there. Virgil moved before he fully realized it, closing the space between them. This time when his arm rose, it didn't strike out, but instead wrapped around Aidan's neck, dragging him forward until he crashed into Virgil. Idly, Virgil thought his brain must have shorted out somewhere along the way, because why else would his mouth be on Aidan's, hungrily trying to gain entrance, seeking more?

Virgil felt Aidan groan and pulled him closer, the hard press of Aidan's cock against his own proof positive this wasn't unwanted. Instinctively, Virgil's hips began to rock against Aidan's, trying to increase the pressure and friction on his own erection begging for attention. Slowly, reality seeped into Virgil's muddled brain. He was making out with another man, and it didn't make him ill. Wasn't it supposed to be wrong? His body sure as hell didn't think it very wrong. But—he couldn't think straight as Aidan's hands found their way under his shirt, callused palms hot and rough as they grabbed for better purchase.

It took considerable effort, but Virgil broke away. He could have sworn Aidan looked hurt, but when Virgil blinked, Aidan was only out of breath and on guard.

Cock throbbing in time to his thumping heart and the taste of Aidan still present on his tongue, Virgil found it difficult to speak. "What are we doing?"

"As you were the one who kissed me that time, Virgil, don't you think you should already know the answer?" Aidan countered, his voice bordering on angry.

"Well, you didn't stop me, did you?"

Aidan sighed. "Why should I stop what I don't want to stop?"

Virgil's heart stopped in mid-beat before thudding along

again. "You didn't want it to stop," he said slowly, hoping the words would make sense.

Nodding, Aidan spoke with great resignation. "I've been thinking about it for a while. Never planned on acting on it. But when you swung at me, I figured I'd give you a reason to be upset with me. When you kissed me back, I decided to go for it."

Virgil had to be dreaming. No way was any of this happening. "You saying you fancy me?" he asked uncertainly.

Aidan looked past him, finding something of interest in the back of the barn, and scratched his head. "Yeah, I suppose that's what I'm saying."

"You suppose? You suppose?" Virgil's voice rose. "Aidan, this is fucking crazy! You can't fancy me. Stuff like this doesn't happen between men."

Aidan shrugged, nonplussed, swinging his gaze back to Virgil's. "It does. And *you* kissed me the second time."

Fuck, why had he kissed Aidan? And Aidan fancying him didn't explain why Virgil had a hard-on that wasn't going away.

"This ain't right."

It would be easy to turn tail, run and pretend this craziness never happened. Any awkwardness would fade with time. Ten years of friendship didn't end over some crazy act.

Aidan seemed to steel himself before speaking. "I feel like a fool for what I'm about to ask. But I'd be an even bigger fool to let this chance slip by."

"Chance at what?"

"Seeing where this leads."

Virgil frowned. "Meaning you want to take things further."

Aidan nodded.

"How much further?"

"That, my friend, is up to you."

Virgil had a real good idea where further led, and somewhere beneath the surprise and disbelief lay plain old curiosity. Maybe he should become an atheist like Uncle Raymond. He wouldn't have to worry about going to hell then, not that Virgil believed much in any of that to begin with. Still some ideas were difficult to get out of your head, regardless of how much or how little you believed them.

Next time Bill Wellington crossed his path, Virgil was going to kill him. With Drea running a very close second.

Stalling, he said, "What if someone walks in? We're done for if anyone catches us." Why couldn't he say no?

"No one's going to walk in. Everyone's too busy getting ready for the festival."

Virgil couldn't believe he was even considering it. "Supposing I say yes, and we see where curiosity leads us." He fidgeted, running his hands through his hair. "Either of us has the right to call it quits if he doesn't like where it's going. Agreed?"

"If you aren't comfortable, Virgil, we stop here. I won't hate you, honestly."

"So you've really thought about you and me?" Virgil looked at his friend, seeing the same Aidan he'd known for a decade.

Aidan closed the small distance between them and pushed Virgil back against the nearby support post as their mouths met again, Aidan laying claim with unchecked hunger. It was the first blatantly aggressive move Virgil could ever recall Aidan making. On the very rare occasions they did come to blows, Virgil always made the first move. Aidan more often than not kicked his ass in the end, but he never initiated. That alone overwhelmed Virgil.

When Aidan's palm pressed firm and knowing against

Virgil's erection, Virgil suddenly forgot all about overwhelming and strange as his hips arched up into the touch. Virgil wrapped his left hand around Aidan's neck, pulling him closer, deepening the kiss. It really didn't differ much from kissing a woman. A little rougher maybe, with the faint hint of stubble, but otherwise fairly similar.

Aidan's hand moved upward, working open the fastening of his pants before slipping inside. Breaking the kiss, Virgil spoke. "Fuck, Aidan, what—" He groaned, low and guttural, as Aidan took his cock in hand, a hand that didn't feel all that different from Virgil's own. Large, warm, callused.

Acting before thinking could get in the way, Virgil reciprocated, popping open the fly of Aidan's jeans and reaching inside. What he encountered was, well, familiar. Had one of his own, didn't he? Besides the fact that Aidan was involved, it was no different than getting himself off, right? The same smooth hardness as when he took his own cock in hand, maybe a bit thicker but... He kissed Aidan again to clear his mind, or possibly fog it up some more. Wouldn't do to think too much.

He kept pace with Aidan, fast, tight strokes running from base to head over and over again. His teeth clamped down on Aidan's lower lip as he came in quick, jerky spurts, the faint taste of copper barely making it through his perception. Aidan collapsed heavily against him after his own release, and they stood supporting each other as they came down, breathing ragged. That was...Virgil wasn't quite sure what it was, aside from being among the more memorable times he'd gotten off. And not in a bad way.

Aidan stepped back finally, refastening his pants and not quite looking at Virgil. It took him a moment, but Virgil soon followed suit. One of them needed to speak, to head off the inevitable awkwardness that would follow.

"Bet you wish I just hauled off and slugged you, huh?" Aidan studied the rafters.

To add another level of strangeness to the whole affair, Virgil didn't know. A fistfight would have been a hell of a lot easier to deal with. And while he wasn't completely okay with what happened, he wasn't not okay with it, either.

"At least that I can wrap my head around. This?" He shrugged. Then he noticed the lower half of his shirt had a sizeable wet spot, not all of which would be concealed when he tucked it in. And naturally the day had been too nice to wear a jacket. He couldn't go back to town like this. He glanced up at Aidan. "Got a shirt you can spare?"

"Fortunately, Ma just did the wash. Be back in a minute," he replied with a sheepish grin before ducking out of the barn.

Looked like there'd be no pretending this didn't happen.

�☙

But it did, and they behaved awkwardly around each other for a while. Eventually, things went back to normal. Until the following spring when it happened again. Virgil couldn't remember the details of how, only that he'd been thinking about Aidan more and more as the weeks went by. The second time he could definitely blame on his uncle. If Uncle Raymond didn't insist on quarterly visits to Madam Violet's house, the encounter with Aidan would have been just a one-time occurrence. But lying there after he and Madam Violet's star girl, Penny, finished, he felt unsatisfied. Drea had been busy when he'd returned to Morton's Pointe, which left him and Aidan alone. Aidan had met the advance with more relief than surprise.

After that, they came together fairly regularly, often in

Uncle Raymond's stables or carriage house or the Morrison barn, a few times in his uncle's house...always making certain no one would accidentally walk in on them. Drea almost caught them the first time Aidan took him from behind. Five minutes sooner and she would have. As it was, they barely managed to get themselves looking decent before she found them in the barn loft.

It all went smoothly after that, until Aidan went and gave Drea Great-Gran Morrison's ring. They'd both fancied her since she could be fancied, but there had been an unspoken agreement of sorts between them never to cross that line. It could be partly why they'd taken up with each other to begin with. He couldn't say at this point. But facts remained. Aidan made his fool move so Virgil made his, fucking Drea like he'd dreamed about when he wasn't dreaming about fucking Aidan. And fucking Drea was the first time he had been satisfied by a woman since he and Aidan started fooling around with each other.

So, their relationship was in a shambles, and resolving it wasn't going to happen anytime soon, with him and Aidan heading off to Europe tomorrow by way of Chicago and New York.

Speaking of shipping out, he still needed to pack his clothes. No use standing there worrying over what couldn't be helped.

Chapter Three

They were nearly an hour out of Morton's Pointe before Virgil spoke.

"What were you thinking?" he asked without preamble.

It surprised Aidan that his friend had managed to hold out this long without asking after his motivations for giving Drea Great-Gran Morrison's ring. Actually, he was more surprised that Virgil didn't lay him out flat while they had been waiting for the train in the gray predawn. But the three of them had been so busy *not* talking to each other that there really hadn't been the opportunity for confrontation.

The weighty silence in Drea's father's delivery truck when she and Virgil picked him up that morning had told Aidan all he needed to know. Neither Virgil nor Drea were ones to carry their anger in silence. Usually. When they did, it was a very bad sign. Then there was the fact that neither had been able to look at him.

As for the parting itself, when the train finally arrived, an observer would have thought the three of them were little better than strangers. An awkward hug from Drea with a mumbled, "Don't get yourselves killed", before she walked away was about all the interaction that had taken place.

Aidan could only blame himself. His reason for enlisting was far from altruistic. It provided an easy way out of Morton's

Pointe. Plus, he would hopefully be able to set aside enough with his pay to stay off the family farm. Maybe even get a foot in the door at one of the state universities. Risking life and limb seemed like a small price to pay for the opportunity at a life better than that of his parents or siblings. He wasn't aiming for the big city, just a change of scene. Enough to live in a little place in the town proper. There was always factory work, but that wasn't any different from farm life. Up before the sun and bone tired by the time you got home. Never changing, every day more of the same. He needed more out of life than that.

The daily drudgery of farm work had driven him to become such an avid reader over the years, for escape as much as for education. A habit well worth the numerous beatings from his father for neglecting his chores; fortunately, by the age of thirteen, those stopped when his father realized Aidan wouldn't change. As long as he put forth a decent effort with daily chores around the home and yard, his father let him be with regards to the more involved farm work out in the fields. His brothers were another matter, until after he licked Robert, the eldest, in that fight the summer he turned fourteen. When the baby of the family took down one of his older brothers, it earned him some peace.

A rough shove of his shoulder brought Aidan back to the present. He looked over to see Virgil glowering at him, gray eyes a storm of anger and frustration. Aidan felt his cock twitch. Virgil in a temper had always attracted Aidan. All fire and fury and...Aidan willed the thoughts away. Not a place he needed to be going.

"It's going to be a damned long war if you plan on ignoring me, Aidan."

Aidan sighed. "You want to know why I gave Drea the ring. Well, Virgil, I don't know for certain myself to give a good enough answer." It had been a quick, instinctive, act-before-he-

31

thought-about-it-too-much decision. This would be the first time the three of them had spent any great length of time away from each other. "I did it because I want her to still be there when we get back."

Virgil shook his head as if trying to wrap his head around what Aidan said. "So you proposed marriage to our girl because you wanted her to stick around?"

"I didn't actually propose. Just gave her the ring and left," Aidan admitted sheepishly. "Pretty chickenshit way of handling it."

Virgil snorted. "Chickenshit is certainly one way to describe it." Then a bit more sober, he added, "That's not like you, Aidan. I'm supposed to be the asshole, remember?"

"Thought I'd try the role on for size. You can have it back," he joked half-heartedly.

"I've never been all that attached to it." Virgil smiled.

They lapsed into silence. If they'd taken a later train, there would at least have been the buzz of surrounding conversation to accompany the dull clang of metal as the car rolled along.

Not five minutes passed before Aidan couldn't take the quiet anymore. Deciding to risk a fight for the sake of conversation, he asked evenly, "Is that why you fucked, Drea, because I gave her the ring?"

Virgil's face contained a mixture of surprise and not-surprise. "That obvious, is it?"

"Well, I know how you and Drea get when you fight, and this wasn't like that," Aidan replied. "Reminded me of how you and I acted after that first time."

"There's some déjà vu, I'll admit," Virgil agreed. "I really should think twice before kissing people I'm pissed at."

"With your track record, that might not be such a bad

idea."

"No, probably not." He leaned back in the seat and studied the roof of the car. "It started mostly because I was pissed at you for being an idiot for pulling that fool stunt and her because she didn't throw it back in your face. And since things were already such a godawful mess, why the hell not? Guess I couldn't let you have the role of asshole, after all."

"You're a true friend, Virgil," Aidan said wryly. It was none of his business, but he asked anyway, "How was it?"

Virgil didn't reply right away. When he did, he said softly, "Better than I ever imagined."

"Reality generally is. Not quite what you expect, but better at the same time." He thought back to when he'd first kissed Virgil and Virgil had kissed him back. Never in a million years had he expected it, let alone that it might keep on. But it had and...now what? He'd asked Drea to marry him, essentially, and Virgil had fucked her. They were heading off to war together, but it wasn't like relations between them would continue. They couldn't. Maybe by the time Virgil and he came back, things would settle themselves. He doubted it, but it was a nice thought, nonetheless.

Too caught up in his own thoughts, Aidan didn't realize that Virgil had spoken.

"What was that?"

"I asked if you ever thought about telling Drea about us."

"Telling her? Yeah, I've considered it," he said slowly. "I've had nightmares about it. Well, her finding out. And as much as I've never liked keeping anything from her, I'd rather never know how she'd react. Though I think she'd be most upset about having been kept in the dark over us...fucking." Aidan had always had difficulty calling what they did fucking. That's what it was, but not. He thought there had to be a better word for it that wasn't either technical or flowery. Though, he had yet to come across it.

Stretching, Virgil said, "I'm surprised she's never caught on. Or caught us. Especially that first spring."

"We were lucky no one caught us that spring." Aidan remembered the haze of lust and heated fumblings that colored that time. It had been so new and unlike any experience he'd had before. And probably all the more consuming for the fact he never thought it would happen.

His attraction to Virgil was a secret he'd harbored since...he couldn't even remember when it started.

And then there was Drea. His attraction to and feelings for Virgil made a hell of a lot more sense. It wasn't that he found Drea unappealing—she'd been the cause of too many hard-ons and wet dreams for him not to admit he desired her. But she also intimidated him. He admired her strength and stubbornness, but he never felt equal to her. She wasn't all that different in temperament or personality from Virgil, but something about her held him back from considering any relationship beyond friendship. Until he'd given her Great-Gran Morrison's ring out of fear of returning and finding her no longer able to be a part of his life in any way.

"I couldn't bear the thought of her winding up with Bill Wellington," he muttered to himself.

He heard Virgil chuckle beside him. "And here I didn't think that bothered you half as much as me."

"Neither did I. But you know he still keeps coming back no matter how many times she brushes him off. She said yes to him once."

"Yeah, to piss me off and get attention from us both. But then she didn't shut up for more than a month about how boring it was."

"Two years, Virgil, and he hasn't given up yet."

"And you took care of that pretty well, don't you think?" Virgil's eyebrow quirked up.

"I don't know what I was thinking," Aidan groaned. "Maybe I'll get killed, then it won't matter."

"Don't you dare joke about that," Virgil snapped.

Aidan looked at his friend in surprise. "Virgil, I didn't mean it like that."

Tension surrounded Virgil. "We're going over together, and we're coming back together. Alive," he said with finality.

It really wasn't a joking matter. "I don't think I ever thanked you for this. For coming with me."

Virgil shrugged, relaxing somewhat. "Gets me away from Uncle Raymond for a bit. And it's not like I could let you go alone."

"I appreciate it." Then he attempted to lighten the mood again. "Do you think if we're gone long enough, she'll forget about the whole ring debacle?"

Virgil's lips curled in amusement. "We are talking about the same Drea Samuels, right?"

"A man can hope." Aidan wished that he could turn back the clock before things got so complicated. But that'd be going back a long ways. Nothing to do but wait until they returned and hope he figured out how to fix his blunder between now and then.

Chapter Four

The puddles shivered with the impact of artillery fire in the distance. It was a good ways off today. Two miles maybe. Yesterday had been under a mile and that was too close for comfort. Aidan had gotten used to the near constant thudding of not-so-far-off guns, the hum that seemed to permeate the ground and air. While he didn't exactly like it, he would take the distant rumbling over the teeth-rattling impact of the previous morning.

He settled onto an overturned crate, barely damp and almost clean, and pulled out the letter he'd been trying to write to Drea for the past week. There were already three separate dates with a couple sentences beneath each. War wasn't conducive to letter writing. Or much else, for that matter. He smirked.

Sept. 7th

No rain today. I think it might even be less muddy. Of all the useful skills they taught us, dealing with soul-sucking muck wasn't one of them. All right, so "soul-sucking" is a bit extreme. Virgil told me to stop being so damned poetic when I said that out loud the other day. Me, poetic, that's a laugh. You remember the one time I attempted to be poetic. Even Robert still mocks me about the poem, and he's my responsible and mature brother. I tried burning it, but the twins salvaged it and love to pull it out every so often to remind me how foolish I was at thirteen. I've started to realize I'm not all that wiser at twenty-one.

Aidan tapped his pen. In the previous two letters he'd sent Drea, he hadn't mentioned the ring. Mentioning it now didn't feel right, either. But if he kept putting it off, would he ever get around to it?

A loud thud jarred him from his thoughts. The Germans were advancing again. Great.

The break the sergeant promised us is looking to be shorter than expected. At least we're not constantly on the move like we were the first few weeks. We slept somewhere else every night. Now it's every other night.

I am seeing plenty of the French countryside. It's even kind of beautiful, mud and all. France, however, doesn't hold a candle to northern Michigan. Though, not much does. We got spoiled growing up where we did.

Speaking of home, it must be getting quiet again with all the summer people boarding up their homes and heading back to the cities. Morton's Pointe always seems next door to a ghost town when the tourists leave, but it gives the locals a few weeks to enjoy the remaining weather in peace.

Ma says that—

"Trying to write Drea again?"

Aidan's pen scratched across the page at Virgil's voice. Aidan glared up at his friend. "Trying is right. But I did manage more than a couple sentences this time."

Virgil peered over Aidan's shoulder. "You know, if you

37

didn't keep bringing that poem up, people would forget about it like you claim you want them to. Though," he mused, "'soul-sucking muck' is a vast improvement over the 'pools of Arctic'...what word did you use again?"

"'Enchantment'," Aidan mumbled. Virgil was right, he only had himself to blame.

"You made some connection between snow and skin, didn't you?" Virgil's lips twitched in amusement.

Aidan wondered if maybe he shouldn't just tear up the letter now. "I was reading *The Call of the Wild* at the time. It had a big influence, what can I say?"

Virgil chuckled and nudged Aidan over so they could share the crate.

"You know," Virgil spoke quietly, "it wasn't until a few years ago that I figured out the poem was about me as well as Drea."

In spite of the flush of embarrassment he felt, Aidan's smile was genuine. "Yeah, well, you've always been a bit slow on the uptake."

"Watch it," Virgil warned, but there was fondness in his tone.

The ground shook around them.

"I actually get worried when I don't hear that," Virgil confided. "Strange."

"I used to like silence." Aidan studied the dirt wall. No, not dirt, definitely mud. Dirt implied dryness. And, Lord knew, this place was anything but dry. "Now, though, too quiet makes me jumpy. Maybe because it means they're on the move and we will be soon, too."

"It's not like we thought it would be, is it?"

"No, it's not." Aidan sighed. He gave Virgil an apologetic look. "I'm sorry I dragged you into this mess."

Virgil shrugged. "Don't be. I could have stopped you if I wanted to."

"You wanted to go to war?"

"Want to, no. But I was curious." Virgil glanced up at the gray clouds hanging low and heavy above them. "I'm not that curious anymore."

"Me neither." They couldn't change their situation now. They were here, foolish choice or not, and all they could do was see the war through.

"Come on." Virgil stood.

"What?"

"It's getting near lunch. I want to see if the food's ready yet."

The food was almost as dismal as the scenery. But being cold and wet on a full stomach was better than being cold and wet on an empty one. Lousy food or no.

Aidan folded up the letter and stowed it with his pen in his coat.

"Food sounds great," he agreed.

As they headed back to the makeshift mess, Aidan wondered why he had ever thought signing up for the war was a good idea.

Chapter Five

Drea slammed the paper down in the middle of the accounting book. Her father didn't blink at the sudden outburst. He'd gotten used to her temper over the years.

"Daddy, how could you," she shouted, hurt all too evident in her voice.

Jeb Samuels calmly set aside his spectacles, took a quick glance at the paper, then up at his daughter. "We've been running ads in the *Pointe Post* for ages, Drea. What's the fuss?"

"Fuss? Daddy, this is a help-wanted ad. We don't run help-wanted ads. We don't need help."

"No, *we* don't. But I will. Eventually. It's best I start training up someone now," he said. "You won't be working in the store forever, Drea."

"What else would I be doing?"

"Taking care of your family, for one thing."

"Taking care—Jesus Christ, Daddy, not again." She sighed in exasperation. "Even if I wanted to get married, there's no one around here who I would marry." Aidan's ring still hung around her neck, but that didn't change her position any. She had no desire to marry, and if she did, the only men she would consider were halfway across the world in France fighting in a goddamned war she was still pissed at them for running off to.

Her father stood, his face coloring. "Watch your tongue, girl. I'll not have you cursing at me. And don't be telling me you won't be getting married. You're too young to be setting your mind against it."

Drea helping out her father in the store had long been a bone of contention between the two of them. Her father firmly stood by the belief that a woman's place was in the home. Unfortunately for him, but lucky for Drea, money had been tight the last few years, and he had been forced to let her help out. He tried to keep her confined to the front of the store and dealing with the customers, but she managed to get her hands on the store account books when he stepped out, learning on the sly what went on behind the scenes. The intricacies of business fascinated her. Considering that she had inherited her stubbornness from her father, there was little hope that he would change his mind and let her take a more active role in running the store, but the hope was still there. As long as it was the two of them.

"But we only just started turning a profit for the year, and it's November. Why do you want to go and throw that away on help you don't need yet?" she argued.

Her father actually growled. "Goddamn it, Drea, how many times do I have to tell you to keep your nose out of the books? You have no business poking around in them!"

He couldn't get much angrier, so she forged ahead. "If you'd let me poke around in them, I could tell you half a dozen ways you could cut back on some of your expenses."

"I won't have my daughter telling me how to run my business."

"Why do you have to be so stubborn? I could really help you out here if you'd give me a chance." The faintest hint of pleading entered her voice. "Please, Daddy, I—"

41

"Go home, Drea," he said with dangerous calm. "I haven't raised my hand to you since you were seven, don't make me do it now."

With great effort, she held her tongue, turned on her heel and walked out, barely pausing to grab her coat from the hook. If it were anyone but her father, Drea would have stood her ground and pushed until she couldn't push any more. But Jeb Samuels was an obstinate old fool who wouldn't budge unless he decided to.

She got halfway home before her anger got the better of her. Old Lady Foster's sugar maple suffered the brunt of it. Not that it helped much when she stubbed her toe on the damned tree. The fine mist of snow raining down from the branches didn't improve matters any.

"Fuck!" she screamed.

She would have given anything to have Virgil and Aidan around right then. She could rage at Virgil and not risk a stubbed toe, and Aidan would calmly listen, which would eventually settle her down. But they weren't here. She'd barely managed to make it the past four months without them. How she'd last the rest of the war was beyond her.

Not until she glanced down at her coat did Drea realize she was crying. Angrily rubbing the tears away, she continued on, the chill November wind even more bitter cold against the dampness. First a stubbed toe and now tears. She'd be lucky to make it out of town in one piece.

ଓ

Her father didn't come home that night, but that didn't surprise her. It wasn't out of the ordinary for him to stay in the apartment above the store if he wound up working late. She decided to take breakfast in town for him as a peace offering of sorts, but a knock at the front door interrupted her preparations.

"If that's Johnny Miles about his damn mongrel gone missing again," she grumbled as she made her way to the door. Her bad mood quickly dissipated when she saw Aidan's brother Brian on the other side. "Brian, what brings you—" Her voice and smile quickly disappeared when she saw his face. God, no.

"I'm sorry, Drea. It's your father, he..."

Drea stopped listening. She was too relieved to pay any attention to what else Brian had to say. This wasn't about Aidan. He was still alive. But once the relief passed, her brain caught up to what Brian had said. "Daddy?" she asked uneasily.

Brian swallowed hard, his Adam's apple bobbing with the effort. "Gladys North found him this morning. It was too late for the doctor to help him."

"Oh," she said, feeling as if she were outside herself, watching a play. "Oh," she repeated, too numb to do more than stand there dumbly while she waited for it to start to make sense.

Chapter Six

Virgil was enjoying all that France had to offer. Their unit had come upon the quiet little village of Deuxoreilles after a particularly brutal week of fighting, nearly thirty men dead, and the commanders had decided to let them celebrate Christmas a bit early, rest up a few days away from the trenches before moving on to a new set. Rest which took the form of an abundance of locally produced red wine and the pleasure of many eager young village girls.

Well into his second bottle of wine, he currently had a server named Yvette perched on his lap promising all kinds of wicked delights, almost none of which he understood due to his lack of motivation to learn the French language. Aidan had nearly mastered the language by their second month. Unfortunately, he wasn't around to help Virgil at present.

Or hadn't been until now. Virgil spotted his friend by the inn entrance.

"*Pardon moi, un moment.*" Lifting the girl off his lap, he got up to greet Aidan who met him halfway. "About time you showed up. I thought I was going to have to tie you up and drag you here." The last few words trailed off into silence as he caught sight of Aidan's pale, devastated face. "Aidan, what happened?"

Aidan shook his head but remained silent.

Scouting the bar area, Virgil found an abandoned table toward the back and led Aidan there, gently pushing him into a seat.

"I can't help if you won't tell me what happened." He turned a chair backward and sat opposite his friend.

Reaching in his pocket, Aidan handed over a muddy, battered envelope. "We should have been there," he said hoarsely, not seeing Virgil.

He quickly glanced at the postmark; it was from home, well over a month ago. With growing dread, he removed the letter. Aidan's ma kept her words as succinct on paper as she did in person. Ellen Morrison was born to not let anything go to waste, be it food, words or emotion. If he didn't know her as well as he did, the letter would have seemed cold and distant, but it was downright distraught for her, with the bit that mattered anyway. Drea's old man had up and died on her. No warning. Heart attack, according to Doc MacMurray.

"Oh, fuck," Virgil breathed.

"She needs us, and we aren't there," Aidan stated, voice strained so tight that it was liable to shatter at the next word. "We're all she has, clear across the world and more likely to die than not."

"Aidan—"

"We lost thirty of the unit like"—he snapped his fingers—"that. Gone. God, Virgil, we're fools. She was right to be pissed at us. We have no business being over here. None."

For the first time in all the years they'd known each other, Virgil found himself having to be the calm one while Aidan lost it. He didn't care for it.

"It's shitty, Aidan, real shitty, but there's nothing to be done," Virgil stated evenly. "Yeah, we should be there for her. And we will be when we get back. Right now, though, we're stuck here and have to make the most of it. Drea's tough, she'll make it through this."

Aidan wasn't listening; he was caught up in his own fugue. "It's all my fault. We'd still be back there, if it wasn't for me. But no, I'm so goddamned determined to get off the farm that I can't see beyond my own nose half the time. The only reason you're here is because I am." Lightning quick, his hand clamped on Virgil's arm. "Why in the hell didn't you talk me out of this?"

Aidan's words bordered on hysterical. Usually, he was the voice of reason. He didn't fall apart. But he was. What in the hell was Virgil supposed to do? He waved over Yvette, praying the inn had something stronger than red wine.

Calm suddenly replaced Aidan's hysteria. "You should have stayed home, Virgil. There was no sense in both of us coming over here to get killed. And we will, you know," Aidan said with the reserved calm of a person who's decided that the worst will happen and he might as well accept it. "We're going to die over here, fighting in this fucking war neither of us cares about, rotting in this damned mud and forgotten."

Yvette interrupted before Virgil could reply, which was fine by him since he didn't know what to say.

"Ah, Virgil, something to drink, *non?*" Her eyes flickered warily toward Aidan, but the smile never faltered.

"*Oui.* But stronger than wine. Whiskey? Or vodka maybe?" He needed alcohol that would hit Aidan quick.

"*Mon pere*, 'e 'as some from before the war. Normally we not sell to soldiers. But for you, I make the exception," she said cheerfully, giving him a wink before heading to the bar.

Virgil grabbed her arm. "One more thing, Yvette. I'll need a room."

"Room? But your camp, it is not close?"

"Yes, very close. But my friend here needs a night out of camp, and so do I."

Yvette looked at Aidan again, eyebrows arching up in realization when she spied the letter between them. "Bad news?" Virgil nodded. She patted him on the arm. "You do not worry, Virgil, I will 'andle it."

"What are you doing?" Aidan accused him as Yvette tottered off.

"I decided that we earned a bit of a break out of the cold and mud."

"Virgil, we can't stay here."

"Why not? We're not moving out until the day after tomorrow, and the sergeant owes me one for saving his ass last Monday. We'll get blind drunk and sleep in a real bed. I'm not seeing the downside."

"It's...we can't, all right? I know what you're doing," Aidan said pointedly. "You want to take my mind off of all of this, cheer me up? Don't get a room. Get me a ticket home. There's no escaping this, even for a night. I'll be better off back in camp." He stood abruptly. "I need some time to myself. I'll talk to you tomorrow."

Virgil jumped to his feet, knocking his chair over in the process. If he let Aidan walk away, the man was likely to do something incredibly foolish. Virgil didn't want that on his head.

He grabbed Aidan's jacket front. "You're staying here," he warned.

"Virgil, do you want to make a scene?" Aidan asked, his voice oddly quiet.

"If that's what it takes to keep you from walking out that door, yeah, that's what I aim to do."

Aidan nodded. Then Virgil saw stars as Aidan's fist collided with the side of his face.

"Fuck!" He shook his head, dazed, but still held onto Aidan's shirt. "Have you gone crazy?"

"You're the one who insisted on making this a scene."

Virgil resisted the urge to shake his friend. "Goddamn it, Aidan," he growled. "I know you're upset, but that's no reason to take it out on me."

"Isn't that what you always do?" Aidan replied, nonplussed.

Virgil felt his blood rise. "Fuck you." He swung.

And missed. Aidan ducked and struck again.

To hell with it. He tackled Aidan to the dirty wooden floorboards, effectively pinning him there.

"Get off, Virgil," Aidan yelled, struggling.

"Not until you settle down and stop acting like...well, me."

Virgil felt someone behind him and spared a glance back to see Barry Miller, a private in their unit from Wisconsin. "Need a hand, Virgil?"

"Nah. Ain't nothing I can't handle. Thanks, though."

"I'll keep the others out of your way then." Barry headed back to where the other soldiers were starting to gather.

"Get off of me," Aidan snarled.

"Only if you promise not to run or take another swing at me."

Aidan took a deep breath and let it out. "All right. But don't expect me to be happy about it."

"All I expect is for you to quit making a damned fool of yourself." Virgil got up and brushed himself off. Aidan ignored his proffered hand and got up by himself.

"Everything is all right?" Yvette asked, suddenly beside

him, a large clear bottle in her hand.

"Just a minor disagreement," Virgil said pleasantly. "Got that room ready?"

"*Oui.* If you will follow me." Turning quickly on her heel, she forced them to follow.

౷

Aidan waited until Yvette exited the room before speaking. "I want to be left alone. What is so terrible about that?" He hated how whiney he sounded.

Setting the bottle down on the table with deliberate care, Virgil faced him. "What's so terrible is that if I let you run off by yourself, you're going to go do something more stupid than getting us involved in this damned war to begin with."

"I don't need you looking out for me, Virgil," Aidan stated. "I never have."

"I wish I knew what the hell has gotten into you, Aidan. You used to think before you acted. Drea's old man died. It's horrible, and, yes, we should be there for her. But we can't. We're here, and we just have to deal with it. Your running off to camp to mope by yourself ain't going to change that." Virgil sighed as he sat heavily on the bed. "You know what, forget it. Go. You're right. You don't need me looking out for you. Don't know what I was thinking. Sure, you've kept me from being stupid more than once, and I was thinking I'd return the favor but..."

Aidan leaned against the wall and looked at Virgil. His intentions were good, and hell, Aidan would have done the same for Virgil were their situations reversed. But they weren't, and suddenly he had a much better understanding of how

Emery Sanborne

insufferable Virgil must have found him over the years, talking Virgil down after all those fights with Drea.

Drea. Fuck, what was she going to do? Her sister Adelia wouldn't be any help way out in California. Not that they got along. And there was the store to contend with, though Drea probably thought that a blessing in disguise. With her father dead, she could finally have free rein of the place like she'd always wanted.

"You think this damned war is ever going to end?" he asked finally, feeling very, very tired. He made his way over to the small table and the bottle of vodka. Grimacing, he screwed off the top, considered it and took a large swallow. The vodka was tasteless but burnt like fire as it went down. It wouldn't take much to make himself numb. He tilted the bottle toward Virgil. "This idea of yours might not be so crazy after all."

"I have good ones from time to time." Virgil smiled faintly. He got up and walked over to Aidan. Taking the vodka, he said, "Who should we drink to?"

"To Drea?"

Virgil nodded. "To Drea's old man for giving us the toughest girl I ever met. She'll find a way to make it through this." He took a drink and handed it to Aidan, who followed suit.

"To Virgil Craig." Aidan lifted the bottle. "Best friend I ever had and who isn't afraid to let me know when I'm being an ass. Even if he is a bit of a hypocrite in that respect."

Grabbing the bottle from Aidan and drinking before him, Virgil laughed. "Too right."

They continued back and forth, toasting to whatever came into their heads until they neared the last quarter of the bottle. By then they had taken up residence on the bed, leaning against the wall, side-by-side with their now bootless feet dangling over the edge.

50

"In the morning, I am going to hate you," Aidan informed his friend. "Thought I should give you fair warning."

Virgil chuckled. "You won't be hurting that bad in the morning. Vodka's pretty good that way."

Aidan took one last drink from the bottle, then leaned over to set it on the floor. Sitting back up, he saw that Virgil hadn't moved. Breathing even and regular, eyes closed. He could be asleep, but Aidan doubted it. Still, he took full advantage of the moment to study his friend and realized how he had changed in the few short months they'd been overseas. Virgil had never been remotely heavy, but any excess was gone. Everything appeared sharper, more defined. His face was a sculptor's dream, streamlined nose, high cheekbones, square jaw. Power and beauty and...and Aidan had had far too much to drink.

"You know, Aidan, it's not polite to stare, even if the other person seems to be asleep," Virgil murmured, one gray eye peeking open and fixing on Aidan.

Aidan tried unsuccessfully not to blush. He barely managed to control it in the best of circumstances. With close to half a bottle of vodka floating through his veins, it was next to impossible.

To make up for the betrayal of his own face, he tried to keep his voice even. "It's not polite, but you've never minded being looked at. Asleep or awake."

The corner of Virgil's mouth curled up. "This is true. But the real question is, are you going to stare all night, or are you going to act?"

Aidan started to turn, to move in, the response almost automatic, but he stopped himself. He sighed. "We shouldn't, Virgil."

"Why not?" Virgil's head rolled to the side so he looked at Aidan straight on. "Ain't no one but you and me here. And, as

51

opposed to back home, it's almost an absolute guarantee that no one is going to walk in on us."

A valid point, but Aidan found himself hesitating. "We can't keep doing this forever, you know. We're going to have to stop one of these days."

"And you decided that today is that day?" Anger edged Virgil's voice. "You lose all your sense?"

Shrugging, Aidan suddenly felt more sober than he should. "We haven't fucked since before we left home. Maybe that's good."

Virgil's body turned to line up with his head. "What's gotten into you? First the letter, which was understandably upsetting, turned you into a lunatic. Now this? What's going on, Aidan?"

"I don't know." He really didn't. It was suddenly too much. "I don't want to be in this war, but I'm stuck. I want you, but I know I shouldn't. I want to do something with my life, be better than my family, but I know I'm going to be damned lucky to make it out of here alive, let alone in one piece."

Aidan felt the overwhelming sensation of frustration and loss taking hold again. For the majority of his twenty-two years, Aidan had been in control, or had a pretty good idea how to get control back if he didn't have it. But now...

"We're murderers, you know that, Virgil?" he said after a lengthy silence. "In the five months that we've been over here, how many guys like us do you think we've killed? A dozen? Two dozen?" He sounded hysterical, but he couldn't stop himself. "They're not that different from us, are they? Young, with nothing better to do, or looking for a way out, and now they're dead. Why? Because we killed them. Because we're told they're the enemy, and we have to kill them. The mud and the screams and the blood...it's all I dream about. I see it when I'm awake; I see it when I'm asleep. And it's never going to fucking end.

Never. Unless I get cut down on the battlefield. Jesus Christ, Virgil, I'm not ready for that." He grabbed Virgil's shirt desperately. "I don't want to die."

Virgil's hands came to rest on either side of Aidan's head, gentle but firm as they held him in place. "Listen to me, Aidan. You are not going to die. You got that?" Virgil spoke slowly, emphasizing every word. "I'm not going to let that happen. You and me, we'll get through this, and we'll get home in one piece. There ain't no other way it's going to end. Okay, Aidan?"

Aidan couldn't say anything. He tried, swallowing hard, but that only made it worse. Opening his mouth, the only sound that came out was a low, mournful sob. The tears followed shortly thereafter. He barely registered Virgil's arms around him as he collapsed against his friend's chest.

They were never going to make it out of here.

Chapter Seven

Drea had never felt like more of a sham in her life. She wore a new dress fresh from Sears and Roebuck in place of her everyday, locally made fare. All because she wanted to make a good impression with Raymond Craig. A man very unlikely to be impressed by anything she tried as he'd known her since she'd preferred mud to lace as an accessory.

Her nerves were bad enough without adding the dress into the mix. The material was too new, too crisp and the look wasn't normal Morton's Pointe wear, except on the city folk who passed through. She felt like she was playing at being adult, at being a capable businesswoman, at being able to keep things going on her own.

Actually, business wasn't the problem. In the nearly three months since her father's death, she had cut back on the expenses she'd been seeing for years and wanting to correct. Income exceeded outflow every month so far, even if only by a few dollars. The general store could potentially be more than a means of just getting by, if she figured out how to raise the profit margin. She knew expanding the business down the road wasn't out of the question. In order to do that, she would need to have some money set aside so as not to risk shorting herself at the store. Plus, if an emergency arose, the extra money would hopefully provide a decent cushion. Since it was only her now, she needed to keep the future in mind.

That was how she came to be sitting in the bank lobby, dressed fancy and trying to look like she should be taken seriously. She hoped that Virgil's uncle, through the bank and other connections he had, would help her find a buyer for the family homestead. Since her father's death, Drea had only been home a couple of times to pick up items. The apartment over the store was comfortable enough for her needs and driving home and back every day was no more than a waste of time. She didn't live there anymore, what was the point in letting the house sit around empty? It would be one less thing to worry about.

"Drea, this is a pleasure." Raymond Craig's greeting jarred Drea from her thoughts.

Not once in all the years she had known the man had he ever been pleased to see her. Raymond had never hidden his dislike of Virgil's friends, but Drea was always an especial target. She posed a slightly different threat than Aidan. But there was no trace of that dislike now. Maybe because she was here on business. Virgil said that his uncle could be extremely accommodating, friendly almost, to those whom he could potentially profit from.

Composing herself, Drea stood, attempting to use every inch of her five foot nine inches to her advantage and portray herself as confident and capable of holding her ground against him. Which was physically impossible as Raymond possessed the same six-foot-plus, broad-shouldered build of his nephew. A man built to intimidate, he had the personality to back it up.

Tucking the folder of paperwork under her left arm, she held out her right hand. "Good morning, Mr. Craig. It's good to see you again."

Steel eyes, so much like Virgil's but lacking something that

Virgil had, crinkled slightly in practiced amusement as he grasped her hand and brought it to his lips. "Drea, don't you think we're on a first-name basis after all these years?"

Drea felt very much the cornered mouse. Being one of the most influential men in town, not many people were on a first-name basis with Raymond Craig, and none of those select few were below the age of fifty. At least in Morton's Pointe. Perhaps Madam Violet and some of her girls called him Raymond down in Grand Rapids.

"Yes...Raymond, I'm sure we are," she said, attempting to sound more confident than she felt. Drea had never been one to be intimidated by any person, except Virgil's uncle. The man always made her feel that no matter what she did, she would never measure up. Which usually didn't bother her. People could take her or leave her, and she couldn't care less. But this man... Well, he had that effect on everyone. Except Virgil. But Virgil was blood.

"Let's take this into my office, shall we?" Raymond led the way without waiting for a response, leaving her no choice but to follow. It was a quick walk past the handful of tellers and his secretary. He motioned her into his office and waited until she was seated before closing the heavy oak door with an efficient click.

Despite the office's spaciousness, the thick drapes, dark wallpaper and deep, rich mahogany furniture made the space claustrophobic. And it grew even smaller as the seconds ticked past while she waited for Raymond to take a seat across from her.

"We hardly see each other these days, Drea. How have you been getting on? These last few months can't have been easy on you." He shuffled through the papers on his desk.

The attempt to put her at ease only made her more

nervous.

"No." She cleared her throat. "It hasn't. But I've managed. Fortunately, though he hated it, my father made sure I knew my way around the store."

"Very fortunate." Raymond smiled distantly. Focusing on her again, tone still conversational but underlain by all-business, he asked, "So what can I do for you, Drea?"

She gripped the folder on her lap, steeling her nerves. "Well, Raymond, I'm looking to sell the homestead and thought you might be able to help me." She surprised herself with how calm she sounded.

Raymond's eyebrows twitched upward. "Why not consult your father's lawyer? Bernard Rhodes, wasn't it? He is more than capable of assisting you."

"Bernard Rhodes is a good man and a decent lawyer, but he doesn't have a head for business," she said quickly.

"And I do." It was a statement of fact, plain and simple.

"Yes." She swallowed. "Despite your personal opinion of me, I know you'll give me fair trade in business."

"Mixing business with personal opinion isn't wise, if one wishes to do well for oneself." His head tilted to the side as he seemed to assess her. "It doesn't happen often, but I'm beginning to think I underestimated you all these years. You have a good head on your shoulders, Drea. You wouldn't have done as well these past few months if you didn't."

She blinked. Had Raymond complimented her?

He continued on, back to business. "I trust you've brought the deed and property specifications with you?"

Nodding, Drea handed the folder over and waited silently as he went through the documents, jotting down a few notes on the pad of paper beside him. A few minutes later, he closed the

57

portfolio and handed it back to her.

"This may take awhile; the housing market isn't at its best right now. Unless there is some urgent need to sell?"

"No, there's no rush." She looked at him straight on. "But I don't see any reason to hang onto what I don't need."

"Very wise," he agreed. "That's all for now. I'll pass this information along to my associates and see what I can find out. If I have any questions or leads, I can find you at the store?"

"I'm almost always there," she said happily. Her father had often seen the all-consuming nature of running the store as a burden, but not her. Perhaps it was still too new for her, with the store finally completely hers. She liked the store being her life; it was all she had ever wanted. Drea stood, and Raymond followed suit. "Thank you again, Raymond. I appreciate this."

He took her hand and kissed it again. "My pleasure entirely."

Drea left the bank wondering what she had been so nervous about. Maybe she had been wrong about Virgil's uncle all these years.

◌ॐ

She exited the post office a week later preoccupied with opening a letter from Virgil and ran right into Bill Wellington. While he wasn't the last person in the world she wanted to see, he was pretty close to it, mainly because she had no clue how to deal with him. Polite small talk wasn't her strong suit, but she couldn't ignore him, either.

In the two years since he'd asked her to the Harvest Festival, Drea had done everything humanly possible to avoid Bill. He wasn't a bad guy, but he wasn't anybody she wanted to spend time with. It didn't help his case that he made no secret about his interest in courting her. And she'd made no secret about not being interested. It never got through to him. So every time they met, it was awkward, and for some reason she couldn't find it in her to be cruel to him. Maybe she should. Maybe then he'd get the hint.

"How's it going?" he asked after she'd made her apologies and tried to slip away.

"I'm getting by." She forced a smile.

"You know," he said, not quite looking at her, "if you ever need a hand, I'd be more than willing to help. With deliveries. In the store. Anything."

"I've got it under control, Bill." She realized after she spoke how harsh the words sounded. To soften them, she added, "But I'll keep it in mind if life turns crazy. Right now, the store is going fine as a one-woman operation."

"Yeah, all right," he mumbled. He half-looked at her when he took his leave. "Take care of yourself, Drea."

"I will, Bill. Thanks." She touched him lightly on the arm before moving on.

Bill was a good guy. He just wasn't...well, he just wasn't.

Drea looked down at the letter in her hand. The first one she'd received from either of the boys since before her father died. She'd mailed out a quick note a few weeks back, letting them know she was managing pretty well, knowing that Mrs. Morrison had given them a heads-up in one of her biweekly letters. Drea had never been one for correspondence. Then again, she'd never had anyone to correspond with. Except her sister Adelia, but her father had handled that. She tried at first to make an effort with Aidan and Virgil, but she never knew what to say that wouldn't seem boring or pointless. Though the boys weren't much better at keeping in touch. Aidan made up for infrequency with length. Virgil scribbled out maybe half a page to let her know he was alive and gave her a quick summary of things.

Opening the letter, she found two pages, front and back, of Virgil's tight, cramped handwriting. Maybe he had been saving up all these months.

There was the predictable "Sorry to hear about the old man, wish we were there to help..." and some half-hearted comments about the terrible food and how he'd be happy to never see mud again. Then:

You may have heard by the time you get this, or you may not. There's no telling how quickly news gets back home or how much notice the army likes to give families. If not, say nothing to the Morrisons. They'll be told what they need to know when they need to know it. But I only think it's fair that you get a bit of a heads-up that Aidan's on his way home, especially since I'm counting on you to look out for him until I get back. Keep him the hell away from those fool books of his, won't do him any good to go withdrawing from the world and hiding in them musty pages. Drag him into that store to help out, even if you've got everything managed by yourself. Keep him out and about and don't give him lots of time by himself to think. That's what got him where he is right now.

He's still the same old Aidan, don't forget that and don't treat him any different when you see him. See, the war doesn't change you, it takes something from you. Innocence is too fancy a way of putting it, but I guess that's the closest I can get to putting it into words. It makes you forget who you are and that the world ain't all mud and destruction and death and... I wish I was coming home with him. Wish I'd never come in the first place. But I did, and I'm here. I have Uncle Raymond to thank for that. Doesn't matter if your job stinks, it's your job and you get it done. Aidan tried to do that, but this was never his place. It came damn close to breaking him, and that's what nearly got me. But he's not broken, just a bit banged up. The docs have done what they can, but ultimately they can only do so much. They don't know him like we do. Not a one of the three of us likes admitting when we need help, but we're willing to move heaven and hell to help the others when we see the need and they don't.

You were right to be pissed at us, Drea. We were fools coming here. But there's not much we can do about that now. Don't get too used to having Aidan all to yourself. I'm coming home one of these days, even if it does seem like this war could go on forever. It'll end sooner or later, and I'll be home. Then you can rub it in that you told me so.—Virgil.

Drea hadn't realized she'd stopped walking until she reached the end of the letter and found herself standing practically in the middle of the street. Not that there was any traffic to worry about. Morton's Pointe was practically a ghost town in the winter. The country folk kept to the country, and the townsfolk did most of their business on foot. But there were enough people about to notice. Carefully, she folded up the letter and stowed it in her pocket before continuing on to the store.

She didn't know what to think beyond the fact that she was torn between being glad that at least one of them was coming home soon and terrified at how much Aidan had changed. What in the hell would she say to him? How—no, there was no point in getting ahead of herself. She'd deal with what happened when it happened. Aidan was coming home, that was what mattered. Things would be a hell of a lot easier if Virgil were coming too, considering the state of affairs between the three of them when the boys shipped off. But life never gave you what

61

you wanted when you wanted it.

All she knew for certain was she wouldn't be giving him that damned ring back anytime soon. That wasn't a can of worms any of them needed to open.

Chapter Eight

Bitter, stinging cold. Nothing compared to February in Morton's Pointe. Aidan set foot on the snow-scoured platform with an unexpected sense of relief. It felt good to see real winter, with ice and snow and the frozen ground. There was a sharp, sterile clarity that only deep winter provided and no real chance of mud for at least another month, possibly two, if he was lucky. Spring arrived notoriously slow in northern Michigan.

It was good to be home. A day earlier than he was expected was even better.

He'd told his family that he would be getting in the afternoon of the twenty-seventh, because no matter how much he protested, his mother would make certain someone was there to pick him up. Aidan learned long ago that he couldn't win any fight with her, so he had found ways to avoid arguing, such as writing to say he would be coming home a day later than he actually was. The only downside being that he needed to find a way from the station to the farm. As refreshing as the crisp winter air was, he didn't care to walk five miles in it.

He spied Young Portney unloading the daily mail shipment as he had every day for the last forty-odd years. Aidan didn't think Young would mind a bit of company on the two-mile drive into the town proper. The forefathers of Morton's Pointe hadn't anticipated the popularity of the railroad when they'd established the town. The founders picked the location for its proximity to the forest and surrounding lakes, not for its conduciveness to the rail system, which wouldn't reach their neck of the woods until nearly half a century later. At least the town wasn't alone in its plight, and the station served as a hub for a handful of the surrounding towns that had founders also lacking in foresight.

"Well, Aidan Morrison, as I live and breathe. You made it back in one piece," Young greeted him with a cheery grin. "I'm suspecting you'll be needing yourself a ride, am I right?"

Aidan nodded. "Yeah, if it wouldn't trouble you too much."

"Heck, no. Always glad to have company." Young hoisted the bag over his shoulder as if it were nothing. He was a tiny man, wiry and thin, who would never see sixty again, though no one could quite say how old Young was. "I take it you didn't want your folks or brothers here to greet you?"

Young had a way of prying that didn't seem like he was sticking his nose into your business.

"I wanted some time to myself before seeing them," Aidan said as they made their way to Young's rusty pickup.

"Can't fault you none for that. Family's great, but they don't always know when to leave well enough alone, if you get my meaning." Heaving the mail sack into the truck bed, Young pulled open the driver's door and got settled behind the wheel. He waited until Aidan got in and they started pulling away from the station before speaking again. "It's not easy going to war. Don't let no one tell you different. It's not something folks can understand unless they've been there. Them guys that lose a leg or an arm get off easiest. But those of us who aren't marked so clearly have the rougher go of it."

"Thanks, Young." It wasn't perfunctory. Aidan meant it. If anyone in town would understand what he went through, it would be Young. While he hadn't fought in any of the major wars, Young had served with the army for a few years, helping settle the western frontier and keep the peace. He'd been involved in a particularly brutal run-in with a tribe in one of the more lawless territories that led to heavy losses on both sides. Young walked away from the battle with nary a scratch, but two-thirds of his unit had been lost. Details were sketchy at best since Young never talked about it, once he started talking again. He hadn't said a word for nearly two years after his discharge. So coming from Young, the words weren't just empty comfort.

Aidan took his leave of Young at the post office, despite the man's offer of a ride out to the farm if he was willing to stick around for an hour or two while Young got the mail sorted. He needed to see someone else before going home.

Drea didn't look up when he entered the shop, too busy ringing up a customer to do more than shout out a courteous, "Be right with you."

Aidan moved toward the back of the shop, pretending to be interested in the stacks of canned food, searching for courage in the orderly rows. Drea was the person he was most nervous to see again. Brief, friendly letters aside, he had no clue were they stood with each other following his idiot move of giving her Great-Gran's ring before he left.

"Sorry about the wait. Is there something I can help you find?"

Aidan turned slowly and faced her. "Hey, Drea."

Another girl might have gotten teary or thrown herself in his arms. But not Drea. She stood there, eyes widening briefly in surprise. Surprise was quickly replaced by relief and finally suspicion.

"You were supposed to arrive tomorrow," she chastised, the

barest hint of amusement in her tone.

"I changed my mind," he replied simply.

Drea shook her head with a faint, knowing smile. "You never had any intention of taking the train in tomorrow."

"No."

"Your ma's going to be pissed. She hates surprises."

"I figured she'd let it slide this once."

"This is *your* mother we're talking about here."

He couldn't help but grin. "She'll get over it like she always does."

One of her eyebrows arched up in the patented Drea Samuels' look that said clearly, "You are a complete and utter idiot."

It was good to know that in spite of all that had happened in the last eight months, some things would never change.

"Come on," she said, starting toward the front of the store. When he didn't follow, she sighed. "I'm taking you home, Aidan. You might not mind your ma being in a rage at you, but I sure don't want her directing any of that toward me."

"Ten minutes and you're already tired of me?" he joked. But the delay in her response worried him. The emotion that flitted across her face wasn't there long enough for him to pin it down.

"You know it takes at least fifteen minutes for me to get sick of you," she teased. But the brief silence that had fallen dampened any humor.

"Drea, what—"

"Come on, Aidan, before Gladys North decides she needs more cat food."

She left him no choice but to follow. Maybe things did change after all.

C3

She thought she was prepared to see him again. This was Aidan, who she had known for practically ever. But when she saw him standing in her store, realized that this wasn't just any customer...well, she had been very glad his back had been to her.

Virgil told her to treat Aidan like always, something she hadn't realized was next to impossible until Aidan showed up that afternoon. Things had changed before he left. Things had changed even more while he was gone. And now that he was back, they sure as hell were going to change some more. It didn't mean she wasn't going to pretend otherwise.

She kept conversation light and neutral on the way out to the farm, nothing personal, just gossip about the townsfolk, which really wasn't all that abundant when one had to rely solely upon that as a subject for discussion. But soon enough they got to his folks' place, and there was enough bustle from Aidan's mother and the rest of his family for Drea to fade into the background and delay the inevitable awkwardness until a later time.

She stayed for dinner but took her leave when she saw that Aidan was well settled. He needed to be with his family right now, and Drea needed the time to figure out how she was going to handle him.

She barely reached the delivery truck before Aidan caught up with her.

"If I didn't know any better, I'd think you were trying to get away from me." He came around to lean against the hood of the truck.

There were times she wished he didn't know her so well. "I

thought you should probably have time alone with your family. There are going to be more than enough chances for us to see each other."

"I'm not going to fall apart on you, Drea, if that's what you're so afraid of." He sounded hurt.

That cut deep. "Christ, Aidan, do you think so little of me?"

"Well, I don't quite know what to think right now. About a lot of things," he admitted.

"You aren't alone on that." Drea sighed, leaning back against the truck door. Instead of looking at Aidan, she studied the crystal clear night sky. "I can't even begin to imagine what you saw over there, and I don't know as I'd want to. Let alone what you've been through. But it doesn't mean I think any less of you. Hell, I admire you all the more for coming back like this." She paused, searching the darkness for her next words. Finally, she turned her head to look at him. "I don't know how to act around you. Not because of the war, but because neither of us is who we were before. I don't even know how to act around myself half the time anymore."

Aidan slowly drew up next to her and took her right hand up in his left. "I never got the chance to say how sorry I was to hear about your old man."

She shrugged, enjoying the solid strength of him next to her and the small amount of warmth he provided in the chilly night. "Honestly, I'd be lying if I didn't say a tiny piece of me wasn't happy about it. I loved Daddy, don't get me wrong," she rushed, "but I finally have free rein of the store like I always wanted. And I'd rather he went all sudden like he did than grow frail from age or disease. But I do miss him. Left me with no one but myself to fight with, and where's the fun in that?" she joked lamely.

"So you've been managing pretty well, then?"

"Store's easy enough to run. I've known it inside out since as long as I can remember. And it's nice being able to do the bookkeeping and not fear Daddy laying into me for the next week if he finds out. It's other stuff that's been a bear to figure out." Drea studied their interlinked hands. "You know I'm selling the house, right?"

He nodded, not commenting.

She used her free hand to tuck away the stray strands of hair whispering in her face, before continuing. "I've been living at the store since Daddy died, and keeping the house for sentimental value doesn't make much sense. Besides, having extra money set aside can't hurt, be it for emergencies or doing something with the store." Frowning, she grew thoughtful. "No wonder Raymond was so impressed with me. Who knew I could be so level-headed and practical?"

"Raymond? As in Raymond Craig, Virgil's uncle?" Aidan looked skeptical.

"I went to him to help me sell. He's not the ogre I thought he was all these years." She grinned at the gobsmacked look on Aidan's face. "I know, me saying something nice about Raymond Craig, who knew?"

"I think you've been alone too long, Drea," he said, his voice mostly teasing.

"Guess it's good you're here to set me right, huh?"

"You're too stubborn for me to set you too right." Then he sobered, squeezing her hand lightly. "It really is good to be back."

She looked at Aidan, really looked at him for the first time since he arrived. He was thinner, the shadows from the dim light making it more apparent, though he would never be skinny by any stretch of the imagination. Maybe he'd finally lost that last bit of baby fat. Aidan had always acted older than her and Virgil, but now he actually looked older. Grown up.

Drea brought her left hand up to cup the side of his face, feeling as well as seeing the change.

"I'm so glad you're home, Aidan," she answered finally. "I missed you, but I didn't realize how much until I saw you again today."

He captured that hand as well.

It struck her then how incredibly intimate this all was, but it didn't make her uncomfortable.

"I know what happened between you and Virgil," he said as if merely commenting on the weather. "Figured it out for myself."

"Oh." If she'd bothered to give the matter any thought at all, she would have been surprised if Aidan *hadn't* figured it out. But... "I don't know what to say."

"You don't have to say anything," he assured her in the easy way he had. "I didn't want there to be more awkwardness between us than there already is. Especially after I forced that damned ring on you before I left."

Damned ring. Drea was aware of the cold press of metal against her chest, light and heavy at the same time. He regretted giving her the ring? Somehow the dismissal hurt more than she thought it should.

"Awkward." She forced a laugh. "Wouldn't be much of a friendship if we let awkward get in the way, right?"

"Right." He looked genuinely happy, relieved almost.

Slowly she withdrew her hands from his, reluctant to lose the contact as much as the warmth they provided. "It's getting late, I should be getting back."

"Big businesswoman have to rise with the sun, I bet," he teased.

"Well, not that early." She kept her voice light. "Don't be a stranger. I'm always happy to have company."

"I'll keep that in mind."

On impulse, she grabbed him for a quick, hard hug. "You don't know how happy I am that you're back. Really," she whispered before pulling away and opening the truck door. Before she got in, she put out an open invitation. "You know, if you're looking for something to do, I could use an extra hand around the store."

"Heavy lifting, huh?" He grinned.

"Pretty much." This time the laugh wasn't forced. "Good night, Aidan."

"Night, Drea." Hitting the hood in a get-going gesture, he turned and headed back to the house.

She waited until Aidan disappeared into the house to start up the truck and head in to town. She found herself wondering, as she navigated the narrow curves, why he hadn't asked for the ring back. But for all the big deal it had been, or seemed to be, it barely warranted a comment in passing. The lack of discussion hurt her and left her feeling very relieved at the same time. In all honesty, Drea didn't know if she wanted to give up the ring at all. She wasn't seriously considering the something he'd given her to consider; she'd just gotten used to having the ring. Best to keep on ignoring it. That was the only safe bet. Maybe figure it out when things settled down. Or never. Never worked very well for her.

Chapter Nine

Aidan showed up at the store not long after opening the next day. Drea hadn't unlocked the door but ten minutes earlier when the bell chimed announcing his arrival.

She smiled. "It hasn't even been twenty-four hours and your ma's already driven you out?"

"Believe it or not, Da did." He didn't seem too upset by the matter. "Said I needed to get out and didn't want to see me back until after sundown. He laughed at me when I told him I planned on helping him around the farm today. Though why I thought he would take me seriously after I've spent the better part of my life trying to avoid doing farm work, I don't know." The corner of his mouth curled in amusement.

"And I expect it's up to me to figure out what to do with you?" she said lightly.

"You're the one who offered. It's not my fault if you didn't expect me to take you up on it so soon."

Drea attempted to appear put out by his unexpected presence, but she was too happy to have him back home and safe. "Well, lucky for you, supplies should be coming in midmorning. That'll keep both of us busy for a while."

"I knew you wanted me for the heavy lifting."

Shaking her head with a grin, she tugged on Aidan's sleeve. "Come on, muscle man. I'll give you the grand tour. I've made a couple changes since you were in here last and don't fancy my system getting messed up."

☙

Drea was glad for the company. There was always enough business to keep the day from crawling, but it helped time pass quicker with someone to talk to during the lulls. And not just any someone, a friend. She'd missed Aidan and Virgil being around, but she didn't realize how much until she got one of them back. What she really hadn't noticed was how isolated she had become, that the store was indeed her life now.

Things soon settled into a routine. Aidan showed up every day around opening, and Drea drove him home when they finished the afternoon deliveries. After the initial excitement of his return passed, folks coming into the store accepted Aidan as much a part of it as Drea was. It wasn't until a Tuesday in late April when he didn't get in until almost noon, having helped his father deliver a new foal, that she realized how much she counted on him being there every day. The store wasn't busier or anything, but Aidan had become a part of daily life there, and it didn't seem right not having him around.

"I managed fine when you weren't here, but I didn't used to know how lonely it got here when it was only me," she said as they made the deliveries later that day.

"Only you? Seems to me like you've got plenty of company. Is it since you took over, or has it always been that busy?"

"Customers aren't company, Aidan."

"I don't know. The way Gladys North likes to go on, she's like company," he teased.

"You wait until she holds you hostage with the exploits of her dozen or so cats, then you'll see how much company she is," Drea groused good-naturedly.

"Gladys is harmless." The humor faded from his voice when he spoke next. "What I don't get is Virgil's uncle coming around like he does. He's not the type of man I see doing his own shopping."

"Raymond has been dropping by to keep me updated on the sale of the homestead. He's not as bad as we thought all these years," she replied, unruffled. "And there's no one better for talking business with. Part of the reason I'm selling the homestead is to have money to set aside for future expansion to the store. And not size-wise, I might expand the services offered. Raymond's a great source to tap for ideas."

"Drea, this is Raymond Craig we're talking about. His own nephew doesn't even speak that favorably about him. You'd be smart to watch him. Especially with any ideas he has for expanding your business ventures." There was a hard set to Aidan's jaw. "And what are you doing being on a first-name basis with him?"

"Is that some sort of crime? What's it matter?" Now she was getting annoyed. If Aidan was touchy about her being on a first-name basis, it was probably best for her not to mention what type of business Raymond had suggested. She wasn't without her own reservations with regards to setting up a speakeasy, if the nation kept up its trend toward temperance. While it was known to bring in a considerable profit, Drea did fine with the store as is. Why risk everything and possibly run afoul of the law if she didn't need to?

Aidan shook his head and sighed, breaking her reverie. "It doesn't much, I suppose. Just be careful around him."

"Of course," she agreed, mainly for the sake of stopping the argument, and focused all her attention on the rocky road leading to the MacKenzie place. She wished she'd insisted on driving today. The conversation would have never happened and she wouldn't be questioning Raymond's motives. Aidan would have been too busy reading to her for them to argue.

On the days Drea drove, Aidan pulled out whatever book he was currently devouring and read out loud to her as she navigated the countryside. He even read to her in the store on the really slow days. She'd never been much on books, but she could almost get why he liked them so much. It reminded her of when they had all been growing up and the lazy summer days in the Morrison hayloft when Aidan would read to her and Virgil, attempting to give them a bit of education in spite of their resistance.

"I'm sorry, Drea. I didn't mean to upset you," Aidan apologized.

"I'm not upset. Though to be on the safe side, I'm doing all the driving from now on. Keep you busy reading to me, then we can't argue. Besides," she added, "I'll never hear the end of that new book any other way."

"I'm not only your pack mule, I'm your entertainment, too," he teased, good mood returning. "So you know, Drea, I only read through the boring parts on my own. I wouldn't cheat you out of the good stuff."

Drea felt the color rise in her cheeks at that. The simple consideration flattered her more than it rightly should, though it was what he'd probably always done. Friendly consideration and nothing more. She turned to look out at the passing countryside. What on earth was wrong with her?

"I hope not," she said as lightly as she could manage, "because I actually like this one."

He chuckled beside her. "Never thought I'd see the day."

She looked back at him then. "What? That I'd admit to liking a book?"

"Yup." For the first time since Aidan got back, he looked genuinely happy.

"Yeah, well, stranger things have happened. Just don't let it get around. I've got a reputation, you know."

"For being a hothead? I don't think this will interfere too much." His lips twitched in spite of his attempts to keep a straight face.

She smacked him on the upper arm, hard enough to make him wince.

"Easy," he laughed. "You know, Drea, for all that you look like a girl, you sure don't hit like one."

"I'll take that as a compliment," she replied proudly. "And if I did hit like a girl, that wouldn't look too good for you and Virgil, who taught me how to hit right in the first place."

The moment she said Virgil's name, mentioning him directly, Drea could feel the good humor that had been restored between her and Aidan evaporate. It wasn't that they avoided talking about Virgil, but his absence was felt enough without drawing more attention to it.

Aidan's look of happy contentment had been replaced by the near-constant drawn and world-weary look he wore so often since his return. His tone remained jovial when he spoke. "There are days I think we taught you a little too well. Leaves us without any advantage over you."

"That's where you're wrong, Aidan. You're the one who's always had the advantage over both Virgil and me. You don't lose control like we do. And you always manage to talk us down, once we stop being stubborn and listen to you."

"I lose control plenty," Aidan murmured quietly as he

pulled the truck over to the side of the road and turned it off. They were still a good distance from the MacKenzie place, so he wasn't stopping for the delivery.

"Aidan, what—"

"You haven't once asked me about what happened over there." He wasn't angry but hurt. "I'm sure Virgil probably filled you in. Still, you haven't said a word. Hell, my family hasn't said a word. Everyone acts like I never went away at all."

"Maybe we're not all that sure how to talk to you about it," Drea admitted. "Let alone that you'd even want to talk about it. It's not that we're pretending nothing happened so much as waiting on you to show us how you want us to handle it."

"You could come right out and ask me." Anger began to creep into his tone. "If I didn't break over there, I sure as hell won't break from a few curious questions here." His voice softened somewhat. "I thought your curiosity would win out over consideration, and I could count on you, at least, to cut through the bullshit and ask."

"You know, it's possible that we're not afraid of hurting you so much as afraid of what you'll tell us."

"Such as what?" he asked curiously, shifting in his seat to lean toward her. "That I'm a murderer? That I shot and killed guys no different from me because they were on the wrong side of some stupid line that doesn't exist?"

This wasn't the Aidan she was used to. She had seen him angry before; he may have had the patience of a saint most times, but even he had his limits. But this wasn't Aidan angry. This was beyond anger. Frustration? Uncertainty? There was a strange light in his normally warm brown eyes that Drea didn't like seeing.

"I thought you were my friend, Drea."

"What do you mean, you thought? Of course, I'm your

friend," she said defensively.

"Then ask me about what happened."

"I..." She stopped, her own frustration finally taking hold. "Aidan, if you're so dead-set on talking, why don't you go ahead and talk? Why should I have to ask? You know I'll always listen."

"Ask me what happened, Drea. Please."

It was the quiet, understated plea in his voice that got her. "All right, Aidan." She hesitated, not all that sure of what exactly to ask him. Well, the direct approach never hurt. "What happened to you over there?"

Relief showed on his face as he sat back. He didn't say a word, seeming to take a sudden intense interest in the steering wheel. When Drea was getting ready to lay into him for making her ask and then not giving her an answer, he did. His voice, normally so rich and varied, sounded hollow, almost dead when he spoke.

"I couldn't cut it." He ran his hands along the steering wheel. "It was easy enough to shut down, go into an almost dreamlike state after that first time coming up out of the trenches, facing the gunfire. You don't think, just act. Do what you need to survive. But even when you're not thinking, you're taking everything in. The blood and the mud and the smoke and the screams are all sharper, more intense. But you don't notice, until after, the way it all lingers, surrounds you."

He lost himself, staring at the bleak, gray-brown farmland around them. Winter was over, but spring was still a ways off. The snow was disappearing by gradual degrees, so hopefully by the time it got warm, there wouldn't be a big melt. He was glad it hadn't been a wet, muddy spring. It meant things wouldn't green up as quick for the lack of rain, but there wouldn't be any

78

mud, either. Aidan remembered he wasn't alone and continued with a quick, apologetic look to Drea. "If you make it through, you come back, joking with the other guys who made it, as if it were only a casual stroll you went on. The reality doesn't hit you for hours, sometimes days later. But you push it down, get past it and get ready for the next time, whether you want to or not. You can only do that for so long before it creeps up on you and won't let you push it down anymore.

"Seeing some of the others in the hospital, I got off pretty lucky in the end." Boy had he ever. "There was this kid, from France. He'd been at the hospital since not long after the war started. The nurses had to do pretty much everything for him; he was like a living doll. Most of the time, they left him to himself, sitting, staring glassily at who knows what. Compared to him, I was fine. What's insomnia compared to complete catatonia?" Though he'd had his fair share of the latter as well, the doctors told him. There was a nearly two-week gap in his memory between the look of naked fear on Virgil's face in the room above that inn and waking up to chrome and dingy white. It still shook him how a person's mind could so completely shut down.

After he'd come around, he didn't sleep more than an hour or so at a time until the doctors cleared him to head home. Only when he was awake had he been able to escape completely. He preferred the harsh, broken reality of the hospital ward to the bleak dreams that came to him.

"Aidan?" Drea asked uncertainly, her hand shaking his arm lightly and breaking him from his reverie.

"Sorry." He gave her a faint smile as he took her hand. "It's easy to get caught up in it, looking back. They told me to keep talking, but it's less difficult to wait for other people to ask, and hope they don't so you can maybe forget it and move on."

"You were right about me being a bad friend. I've never handled you with kid gloves before; I don't know why I started. Except maybe..." She trailed off, her brow furrowed in thought. When she spoke again, she looked at him straight on, the blue of her eyes so brilliant they almost hurt. "So much has happened. So much, and it hasn't even been a year yet since you and Virgil took off. Nothing happened for so long, it's like everything decided to happen at once."

"It was a lot easier when we were younger." Aidan wondered what Drea had done with Great-Gran's ring. He had a feeling she hadn't mentioned it for the same reason he hadn't—that the whole thing would blow over like it never was. It was on the tip of his tongue to broach the subject because now wouldn't be any worse than any other time, but Drea interrupted him.

"It's getting late. The MacKenzies will be wondering where their groceries are. Not to mention the fact your ma'll have my hide if I have you home late for dinner."

He let go of her hand and started the truck up again. "You always say that, but you know full well she's got a soft spot for you."

"Your ma doesn't have a soft spot for anyone."

"Softer, then."

Drea shook her head, but it didn't hide the faint blush on her cheeks. "Just drive, Aidan."

Chapter Ten

After the mail arrived, Virgil slipped away from camp to read his letters in relative peace. It was something he liked to do, when the unit wasn't on active duty or in a particularly dangerous area. The letters from home were an escape, and he needed to be away from any blatant reminder of what he was trying to escape from. He could see why Aidan had been so attached to his books over the years. Not that Virgil was going to take up serious reading anytime soon, but he now understood the power the written word had to take you away for a bit.

The commotion from the camp reached him while he was finishing reading his weekly letter from Uncle Raymond. His ears perked up as he looked back. There was no gunfire and the shouts sounded like cheers, though at this distance it was difficult to say for sure. Curiosity getting the better of him, Virgil stowed the letter in his jacket and started back. Words from home were great, but whatever was going on in camp had to be more exciting than whatever Uncle Raymond had to say.

Barry nearly ran him down. "Virgil! I've been looking everywhere for you." His mousey hair stood up wildly about his head. "Have you heard?"

The guys running around acting like a bunch of wild idiots distracted Virgil. "Heard what?"

"It's over, Virgil. We're going home!" Barry was practically dancing.

"Home?"

"The war. Done. Over. Finished."

"The war is over?" he said uncertainly, the words feeling foreign on his tongue.

Barry grabbed Virgil's upper arms and shook him. "Yes."

Over. Really over. But it had seemed so endless.

"I think I need to sit down." He sat down hard on the solid, rocky ground.

Barry squatted in front of him. "You okay, Virgil?"

He nodded. "I will be. Give me a minute."

Well, hell. Virgil couldn't think of a time he had ever been so flat-out stunned before in his life.

"It's really over?"

Barry grinned. "That it is, my friend. Germans laid down last night. You do know what this means, don't you?" When Virgil didn't reply, Barry slapped him on the arm. "We could very well be home by Christmas. I'm dying for all of Mom's cooking, but damn, her turkey's what I miss the most."

Virgil knew he should be thrilled, but he couldn't find it in himself to be excited. Sure, he wanted to go home. He didn't belong here in the first place. The only reason he'd joined up was because Aidan had been so dead-set on going. Then Aidan had gone home and left Virgil by himself.

"I've gotten used to this life," he murmured in realization. He looked at Barry. "I know it sounds crazy, but I have. How do you get used to this?"

Some of Barry's excitement faded. "Survival, maybe? Get used to it or go nuts?"

"Maybe." Virgil ran his hand through his hair. "I hate this place, but when I think about leaving it..."

"Ah," Barry said knowingly, joining Virgil on the ground. "You're worried they've moved on without you."

"What? Not at all," he scoffed.

"No? From what you and Aidan told me when we got shipped over here, you two and that Drea were thick as thieves. Never been apart for any stretch of time, have you?"

"But it's not like that between us," he protested, even though things had been moving in the direction Barry implied since Virgil and Aidan had taken up together. And then before they'd left, Aidan had given Drea that ring and Virgil had fucked her. Oh yeah, life was going to be dandy. "Fuck."

"Hey, Virgil, I didn't mean anything by it. Have I ever told you I suck at this?" Barry apologized sheepishly. "Always end up saying the wrong thing."

"It's not your fault. We had problems before we shipped over. But there's nothing to do but deal with it, right?" He paused. "The possibility of getting killed aside, that's what had Drea the most upset. She was afraid that with Aidan and I taking off without her, we'd move on and she'd be left back in the dust. Well, that and we sort of sprung this on her without much warning."

"That, I'm sure, was part of it," Barry agreed as he stood. Brushing himself off, he offered Virgil his hand. "What you say we go join the party? There's never been a better cause."

Virgil took the proffered hand and stood as well. "That, Barry, is the best possible advice. Come on."

Why worry about what he couldn't do anything about, yet. When he got home, things would go how they would. Until then, it was time to celebrate.

Chapter Eleven

"And then there's my Annabelle. Poor dear. After Jasper passed on this summer, she hasn't been the same. Lost that spring in her step, if you know what I mean."

Aidan nodded politely while he wrapped up Gladys North's purchases for the day and made a mental note to never make another bet with Drea. There had been an extra pumpkin pie left over from Thanksgiving dinner that year that he'd sent home with Drea. The next day at the store had been deadly quiet, and she pulled out the pie, cut it in half and bet him the month of December waiting on Gladys North that she could eat her half quicker than him.

Somehow he had managed to forget that Drea had won the pie-eating contest at the county fair three years running. It was how they'd first met. At ten, he had been so impressed by the fact a petite, seven-year-old *girl* had beaten him that he had to get to know her better. He'd seen her at school and in passing, but she was a girl, what good was she for fun? A lot, he discovered. Even if it did earn him a fair amount of teasing from his brothers over taking up with a girl.

"Camilla, now, she's been the queen bee since Annabelle stepped down. Thinks she rules the roost. But Micah keeps her in line most days."

"There's never a dull moment, is there?" he cut her off, keeping his tone as kind as he could manage. Fourteen days down, seventeen to go.

"You don't know the half of it," Gladys exclaimed, bemused as she gathered her purchases. "Best be getting back before they make a complete mess of the place."

Aidan sighed with relief when the door clicked shut behind her. It was his own fault for asking her about the cats one day, attempting to make polite conversation. Now she talked of nothing else.

Sitting heavily on the stool behind the counter, he leaned back and closed his eyes, figuring he earned the right to a quick catnap before Drea got back and they had to go out on the afternoon deliveries.

Aidan was just getting comfortable when the bell over the door clanged wildly. He looked up in time to see Drea slam the door shut. Her eyes were bright and her cheeks flushed as she ran over to him.

"Drea, what on earth—"

"He's coming home!" She shoved the crumpled letter at him.

Snatching the paper, he quickly recognized Virgil's tight, cramped script.

Was hoping to get home by Christmas, but I think the army figured that the war being over was gift enough. Should be there before the middle of January, though. God, I can't wait to be able to stick in one place for more than a couple days at a time. I have no intention of leaving the greater Morton's Pointe area again for a long, long time. Even for Grand Rapids. Uncle Raymond's a big boy, he can go visit Madam Violet's by himself...

Aidan stopped reading and looked at Drea, a slow grin forming on his lips. "He's coming home," he repeated quietly.

"I knew after the Armistice that it was only a matter of time but..." She leaned back with a happy sigh, her elbows resting behind her on the countertop. "It didn't seem real until now, you know?"

He nodded. Life would finally get back to normal. With that realization, some of Aidan's good mood evaporated. But what normal? With all parties present and accounted for, certain ignored issues could no longer be ignored.

"Aidan, what's wrong?" Drea pushed off the counter and came to stand directly in front of him.

"The usual, I got to thinking too much is all." Aidan looked down at his hands.

Drea's fingers ran lightly along his jaw before tugging on his chin to force him to look at her. "You have nothing to feel guilty about. You do know that, right?"

He felt guilty, but it wasn't about leaving Virgil fighting the war when he couldn't cut it. No, Aidan felt guilty because a very small part of him wouldn't have minded Virgil staying gone a little while longer.

His right hand rose and wrapped around the hand that cradled his chin, easing it away but not releasing it. Looking at Drea full-on, he confessed, "A part of me resents Virgil coming home. I've never really had you all to myself except for way back in the beginning, and I discovered I like not sharing you for a change."

Drea's eyes widened, but she eased her reaction with a faint smile. "You ever think that maybe I've liked not sharing you for a change? Being the only girl leaves me feeling like a third wheel sometimes. It doesn't matter how close the three of us are, some things I can't be a part of."

He wondered if she had even the tiniest of suspicions about the *things* he and Virgil had done together. Maybe he should tell her, clear the air. Hell, was it really all that different from what she had done with Virgil? No. And yes. Yes, because it hadn't been a one-time occurrence. One time she'd be fine with. Hopefully. But to know they'd been going at each other behind her back for a couple of years?

"Aidan?" Drea tugged on his hand to get his attention.

Her blue eyes were softer than he'd seen them in a long while. Aidan realized that if he opened his mouth to reply, he'd tell her everything. And if he did that, life would go from good to really bad quicker than he could blink, and worse once Virgil got back.

Instead of talking, he acted. Using the grip on her hand, Aidan tugged Drea forward, pulling her off balance enough to fall against him. Her mouth opened slightly with surprise when he captured it with his own, delving in and laying claim before she could protest.

To his astonishment, she didn't pull away but started kissing him back, her free hand wrapping around his neck to pull him closer.

So soft, he'd forgotten that. And smooth. No faint stubble or firm, resistant flesh. Aidan had grown so used to Virgil that he'd forgotten what kissing a woman was like. What kissing Drea was like, since she was the only girl he'd ever kissed. Even though they'd never kissed like this during their youthful experimentation.

When they pulled apart, Aidan found himself transfixed by Drea's slightly dazed look and her red, swollen lips.

"I want you, Drea," he stated quietly. Not unlike the day he'd kissed Virgil that first time, Aidan decided to take the chance that presented itself, regardless of the response.

She blinked at him, seeming to take considerable effort to process his words. He didn't know what he would do if she said no. Well, that wasn't true. He'd be a gentleman, make an embarrassed apology and slip out to walk home. Maybe stay away for a few days until he got over the humiliation.

"Are you sure?" she asked finally.

That she would actually want to go through with this, he hadn't counted on.

"Yes," he replied.

"Because Virgil had me? Or because you really do want me?" The dazed look had gone. Her gaze was sharp and piercing once more.

"Yes," he said again, "because I want you and have wanted you for a very long time."

She studied him. "All right, then." She pushed off of him and went to the front door, throwing the lock and turning the sign to CLOSED. Then she made her way toward the back of the store, stopping when she realized he hadn't moved. Glancing over her shoulder, she asked, her voice gentle but with the faintest hint of amusement to it, "You coming, Aidan?"

He nodded, getting to his feet and following her. Neither of them said a word as they climbed the steep, narrow staircase leading to the upper floor.

The apartment above the store had served as a home to Drea's parents until her sister had turned three and they moved out to the homestead. So while it wasn't large by any stretch of the imagination, it was homey with all the necessities—parlor, kitchen, bedroom, washroom.

Drea led the way to the bedroom, dropping her coat on the armchair next to the entry. She waited for him to enter the room before closing the door behind them.

"You haven't done this before, have you?" Her question ended on a hopeful note as she tugged at the bottom of the bed quilt to straighten out some unseen wrinkle.

Oh, sure, he had plenty of experience, but none of it involved women. "Not this, no," he replied, happy that while it wasn't the complete truth, it wasn't a lie, either. "Never got around to it."

She looked at him. "Ah, that's going to make this interesting." Smiling sheepishly, she continued, "I was kind of hoping you'd know what to do here because with...the first time"—she shifted uncomfortably from one foot to the other and made a vague waving gesture in the air—"well, it's kind of a blur. I remember it, but I, um, didn't do much?"

It was a rare sight to see Drea Samuels embarrassed or out of sorts.

Taking pity on her, Aidan slowly closed the distance between them. He brought his right hand up and cupped the side of her face, the pink skin slightly feverish to the touch. "The way I see it here, we've got two options," he said soothingly.

"Those being?"

"One, we stop now. There's nothing saying that we have to do this."

"No, there isn't. But you said you wanted this, wanted me," she stated firmly. "And I've been wanting you for a while, Aidan. So that rules out the first one. What's that leave us with?"

He took a deep breath and let it out. "That leaves us with the second option, which is we figure out how this works, together."

"The blind leading the blind, huh?"

"Pretty much," he confirmed.

She nodded once. "Sounds like a plan." She stood on her toes, hands bracing on his shoulders as her lips softly sought out his.

The marked difference from his experience with Virgil struck Aidan again. It wasn't only the feel of Drea that was different, but the way she approached the kiss as well. Hesitant but curious and growing a little bolder as they both relaxed. A gradual build, in sharp contrast to the near instantaneous heat with Virgil. Aidan realized that now wasn't the best time to make comparisons and decided to occupy himself by focusing on the one he was with.

His hands roamed, mapping the terrain of her body. She wasn't curvy, but still had softness to her. Over the years she had joked about being built like a boy, but she was most definitely not one. The easy contour of her waist moved outward toward the gentle prominence of her hips, a welcoming resting place for his exploring hands. But he didn't stop there, venturing back to the gentle swell of her behind barely disguised beneath her simple skirt. There he stopped, fingers digging in slightly, pulling her closer and groaning at the giving press of her stomach against his hardening cock. The action only seemed to encourage her, her kiss growing more demanding as she in turn pulled him closer.

She gradually withdrew to look up at him and inquired, slightly breathless, "Do you want to undress me, or should we take care of ourselves?"

Aidan felt extremely lightheaded as all of his blood flowed rapidly south. Undressing her held a very high appeal, revealing her by subtle degrees with his own hands; however, he had a feeling that he'd be very fortunate to be able to undress himself. At least with that he could rely on years of experience to guide him.

He swallowed hard, fingers flexing where they held her. "Seeing to ourselves is a good idea."

"Maybe next time?" The light note sounded natural, though he could still hear the faint nervousness underneath.

"That sounds promising." Hopefully, he wasn't so terrible that there wouldn't be a next time. But Virgil kept returning, and considering all of his experiences...Aidan shoved thoughts of Virgil aside. Not right now. Virgil wasn't here, and it wouldn't do any good to keep dragging him back in.

"Good." Drea slowly stepped away, making steady work of unfastening the buttons that held her top closed. She stopped, holding the material together when she finished, and flashed him one of her more characteristic teasing looks. "This taking-care-of-ourselves idea kind of involves you taking care of yourself, not standing there watching me."

He ducked his head but wondered why he should be embarrassed having her catch him out. They used to go swimming together every summer; it wasn't like they hadn't already seen all there was to see on each other. Resolved, Aidan unbuttoned his shirt with the same steady pace Drea had. He slipped it off, holding it in his hand for a moment before dropping it on the floor. And, for the first time, he truly appreciated that Drea insisted on keeping the store and apartment as warm as she could manage. Only when you got near the windows could you tell it was winter outside. She said it wasn't a waste as she was just making up for all the years her father had skimped when he was alive. Mr. Samuels hadn't exactly been a skinflint, but you'd be wise to keep your jacket on when you were at the store for any length of time.

Aidan went to remove his undershirt but noticed Drea was still in her shirt.

"Shouldn't you be doing something other than watching me?" he threw back at her.

She grinned, mimicking his actions of slipping her shirt off, holding it, then letting it fall. She moved on to her skirt, waiting for his pants to hit the floor before letting it drop. They continued to alternate one piece at a time until they stood across from each other completely naked.

Aidan found his gaze drawn to Drea's breasts, small, round and looking like they would fit perfectly in his hand. He wondered how heavy they were, and if they were as soft as everything else on her seemed to be.

"It just looks so impossibly big," he heard her murmur. When he glanced up, a faint blush colored her cheeks as she asked, "Doesn't it feel strange when it gets like that?"

He considered his cock, jutting up, hard and dusky, toward his stomach. "Um, a bit maybe, but I'm used to it?" He hadn't really considered it before.

Drea took a hesitant step forward and another before stopping, right hand rising. Worrying her lower lip, she queried, "Would you mind if I touched it?"

Mind? Hell no, he wouldn't mind. But he held himself in check, not wanting to seem too eager. Gently, he grasped her wrist and guided her hand to rest lightly around his shaft. The heat from her hand before she even made contact made his cock twitch in anticipation. When she circled her fingers around, wrapping him completely in her grasp, he thought he very well might lose it then and there. The gesture had a familiarity to it and a very distinct difference at the same time. Maybe because this was his first time with a girl. And not just any girl. Drea.

He guided her hand slowly along the length of his cock, up and back down again. It was complete torture for him, but he enjoyed the situation, watching the way her brow furrowed and relaxed as she processed the sensations.

"It feels like it's alive," she said in a hushed tone. "The way it moves. You can't control that, can you?"

"No. Feels like it has a mind of its own sometimes."

"Glad I don't have to worry about that." She grinned at him.

"Yeah, but you have those." He nodded to her breasts. "Don't they ever get in the way?"

She gave a very unladylike snort. "Hardly. They're not big enough to notice, let alone get in the way."

"They're plenty noticeable," Aidan corrected. He slowly brought his free hand up and carefully cradled one of the pale mounds in his palm. Firm but soft, with a comforting weight to it. Tentatively, he ran his thumb across the dark nipple, the skin crinkling together under his touch. Drea shivered, and he immediately tried to pull his hand away but she held him there.

"Don't stop. It feels...good."

So he didn't stop. And all the while she continued to stroke along his length.

Aidan soon realized he wanted to feel more of her. Abandoning her breast, he slipped his hand down her side. The fine ridges of her ribs gave way to the smooth slope of her waist. He was disappointed when Drea released his cock, but she soon mimicked his explorations, mapping out his body as he was hers.

When their lips came together again, the kiss took on the same roving discovery as their hands. Pulling her closer, deepening the kiss, Aidan reveled in the welcoming crush of her body against his, slight curves giving way and cushioning his hard planes.

"Bed," Drea murmured, breaking away to guide him back

and down with her. Her mouth sought his again, the moment he joined her, hand curling behind his neck.

Settling next to her, he propped himself up on his right side so his left hand could wander unhindered. He lost himself in the feel of her. Moving down from her neck, he encountered a fine metal chain and then the ring. She wore it. Interesting. But he didn't linger, didn't question. Explanations could wait. Continuing on, he moved to her breasts, pleased at how they responded to his touch. How Drea responded. The slight hitch in her breath, the fine spread of goose bumps peppering her skin. He knew her so well, but he'd never known these things. His hand wandered lower, exploring the downy softness of her stomach, gradually moving down into the wiry curls, familiar and different at the same time. No hardness jutted out to greet him, only a gentle sweep leading farther downward.

Drea gasped when his fingers grazed over slick, warm flesh. He almost pulled away on reflex, but she softly encouraged, "Keep going," as her legs opened a bit more. So he did, following the delicate, wet trail as it curved up inside of her. Aidan hesitated again, struck by the familiarity of it all. He knew the heat but not the natural slickness, and there was no resistance as his finger slipped inside the cushiony warmth wrapping around him, enticing him to go deeper. And he did, Drea arching into his touch.

"Amazing." He'd been missing out on something these last few years with Virgil. He withdrew his finger slowly before sliding back in. No resistance.

"Add another." Her quiet request broke into his thoughts.

There was some resistance this time, and he noticed the slight furrow of tension on Drea's face.

When he stopped, she gave him a faint smile of reassurance. "I'll be all right, Aidan." She caressed his cheek.

"Go slow, and I'll be fine."

He went slowly, pressing in, felt her body stretch to accommodate the added finger. He imagined what it would feel like around his cock and could have sworn his heart skipped a beat.

Drea's hand moved from his cheek and down his chest, idly stroking him as he continued his exploration, her fingers tensing every so often as his fingers moved inside of her. She abandoned his chest for his stomach and eventually her hand came to rest lightly around his cock. She kissed him fleetingly. "What do you say we give this a try?"

"Okay." Aidan had a pretty good idea how this worked, had essentially done it countless times with Virgil. Yet he had never really been afraid of hurting Virgil. Drea, on the other hand... "Tell me to stop, and I'll stop. Got that?"

She nodded. "I don't think there's going to be any problem. Don't worry so much."

"Me? Worry?" he joked, carefully removing his fingers. Then, moving over her, he guided himself between her legs. He hesitated. Something else made sex with Drea very different from sex with Virgil. "Maybe we should wait."

"Wait? Why?"

"You were lucky the time you were with Virgil." Even before he finished speaking, he knew he hadn't said it right.

"Meaning..." Anger lay just under her even tone. She was at least giving him a chance to explain himself.

"You didn't get pregnant then. You could now," he rushed on. Years of frank discussions about sex with his friends, often at Drea's insistence, didn't prepare you for frank discussions about sex with one of said friends while on the verge of having sex.

Her laugh surprised him. "I'll be fine," she reassured him as she stroked his cheek. His confusion must have been obvious. "The only bit of useful advice I've ever gotten from Adelia: 'Track your cycles, Drea. A woman needs to be in control.'" She grinned. "It wasn't much use at twelve. Confused the hell out of me. But I figured it out eventually."

"So we're safe?"

"More or less. I may be inexperienced, but I'm no fool."

"I've never thought you were." He bent to give her a quick kiss. "So, I haven't completely killed the mood, have I?"

She shook her head. "Not at all."

"Good." He kissed her again and repositioned himself.

Waiting a heartbeat, then two, he pressed in, liquid fire enveloping head then shaft as he gradually sheathed himself, pausing when he felt her tense, then continuing when she relaxed again. In a way, he was glad to have her responses to focus on, otherwise he wouldn't have made it very far at all. The sensations were so overwhelming. But then he was inside, completely, and closer to Drea than he had ever dreamed. Well, no, he'd dreamed of this. But dreams didn't compare to reality.

Finally trusting himself to speak, he asked, "How are you, Drea?"

Once again, her response wasn't at all what he had expected. She laughed. Well, giggled. Her eyes went wide with apology, and he could see her struggle to stop. It only seemed to make matters worse. She finally pulled herself together.

"God, Aidan, I'm so sorry," she said sincerely and a bit breathless. "I'm fine. I don't know what's wrong with me."

"Nervous."

"Maybe I was, but not anymore." The color rose in her cheeks. "I've probably ruined the whole thing for you, haven't I?

Giggling. I don't giggle." Her fingers combed lightly through his hair as she sighed. "I feel like such an idiot."

"Hey, don't." He dipped his head down to give her a quick, reassuring kiss. "I'd rather that than crying. And it's not like I didn't already know you were strange."

"Watch it," she warned, but the bright grin belied her words.

He was about to say something else but moved, shifting inside her. Drea's sharp gasp cut off any reply he'd had. "Drea?"

She refocused on him. "Do that again."

He did, withdrawing slightly and pressing back in. This time Drea wasn't alone in her response.

"Keep doing that and you won't have to worry about me laughing."

"Yeah?"

"Yeah." She pulled him down so she could reach his mouth, kissing him gently, then shifted her hips beneath him.

Aidan's breath caught. Breaking the kiss, he said, "I don't think you need to worry about me laughing, either."

He felt her smile when he resumed the kiss and started to move in and out of her tight, slick channel. His movements were slow at first, unsure. But as he grew used to the feel of her, his body remembered what to do. He knew this. Different terrain, but the principles were the same. In and out with a steady rhythm, gradually picking up pace. Drea's long legs wrapped around him, opening her up more. Somewhere along the way, Aidan lost all sense of himself, was aware of nothing beyond the feel of Drea sliding and clenching along his length, hips rocking in counterpoint to his. He broke the kiss to nuzzle against her neck, the fine sheen of sweat salty against his lips.

"Faster," he heard her faint plea, fingers digging into his

back muscles, pulling up closer, urging him on.

Faster he went, and harder and deeper, drowning in her, never wanting it to end. The moment he thought never, Aidan's body tensed and released, climax washing over him as he spent himself. He collapsed heavily on top of Drea, not sure that he was ever going to be able to move again.

Chapter Twelve

Drea lay next to a dozing Aidan in the fading afternoon light. It was comforting the way he fit around her, his chest warm and solid against her back, his arm a reassuring weight around her waist. She could get very used to sleeping with him.

Aidan. She'd just had sex with Aidan. Like she'd had sex with Virgil. No, not like, it was very different. Being with Aidan was a world away from her experience with Virgil.

Sex with Virgil had been fierce and heated, not unlike their arguments. It had left her feeling a bit dazed and slightly euphoric, until the guilt took over. Now, with Aidan, she felt relaxed and extremely content. She kept waiting for the guilt to slip in and throw a dark shadow over things. But it wasn't coming. Everything felt very right somehow.

She toyed with the ring around her neck, sliding it idly along the chain. The ring that started it all. If Aidan hadn't given it to her, who knew what would have happened? But why speculate on what couldn't be changed? And why would she change what she didn't regret doing with either of the boys?

On a whim, she worked the clasp around to the front, moving carefully so as not to wake Aidan. Removing the ring from the chain, she held it up in the fading light, the silver taking on the gold tones of the late afternoon. The three plain strands wove together with a simple elegance, separating again and again and again. "Something to consider," Aidan had said before leaving her with it and walking off. And she'd considered it, a lot, but no more so than in the last few months of their comfortable routine. He hadn't asked for it back or made any mention of it, aside from admitting he was an idiot for giving it to her like he did.

Drea slipped the ring onto the third finger of her left hand. Pushing her hand out as far as it would go, she examined the ring, twisting her hand this way and that, watching the stray beams of light wink across the metal strands. It didn't just fit. It fit perfectly. Looked like it belonged there, although she'd never worn a ring before in her life. She had some earbobs of her mother's that she pulled out on special occasions, with a matching string of pearls. Aside from that, she didn't fuss with jewelry. She never felt herself when wearing it and spent the whole time worrying about losing or ruining the pieces.

"Not that you wouldn't look good with a diamond, but I always thought Great-Gran's ring would suit you," murmured Aidan, voice low and still thick with sleep.

Drea blushed at being caught out. Instinctively, she tried to remove the ring, but Aidan captured her wrist, stopping her.

"Leave it on for a second. Please?" he asked, the soft request whispering against her neck. He held her arm out the full length, seeming to mimic her earlier study. "It really does suit you." He eased her arm back and released it. "Have you ever tried the ring on before?"

She shook her head.

"Why now?"

"Curiosity. Maybe?" She honestly didn't know. No, she did know. She just didn't want to look too closely at why she'd done it. Yet. Or ever, if that was possible.

"Is that why you've kept it so long?"

The question was even, neutral, no hint to how he was feeling. While it was easier to talk to Aidan with her back to him, Drea really wanted to know what was going on inside his head. Slowly, she rolled over. His face didn't give her any insight. He had always been good at keeping his feelings close, forcing her to answer him if she wanted the conversation to go any further.

"You never asked for it back," she admitted, unable to look at him directly. She focused on his chin instead and the faint stubble starting to peek out.

"I figured you'd try to give it back to me eventually."

The "try" got her attention, and she met his gaze. There was something there, but she couldn't pin it down. "What do you mean, try?"

"Who else would I give it to? Virgil?" The slight edge to his voice quickly faded. "I gave it to you, Drea, because there's no one else I would ever want to give it to."

"Aidan, I d—"

"Drea, hear me out, all right?" It was more of a command than a request.

Reluctantly, she nodded.

"I'll admit I was a bit panicked when I gave you the ring. I did it partly to make sure you'd still be here if we returned. Didn't want you taking up with Bill Wellington again." He grimaced. "Or anyone else."

She wanted to protest. She'd gone to one event with Bill a little over three years ago and had done everything outside of being flat-out rude to the boy to discourage him. It wasn't her fault Bill couldn't take a hint. Maybe it was a guy thing, since Aidan and Virgil both never got over it, either.

Sighing, she pushed the thoughts aside and didn't

interrupt Aidan as he continued.

"The ring is yours, Drea. I want you to have it. No strings," he added, his dark eyes open and honest. "It doesn't have to mean anything."

"What if I want it to mean something?" she said before she could bite her tongue.

"Something?" he prompted.

"It's not like this is any old ring, Aidan. Your great-gran didn't give it to you to toss away."

"That's not what you said. You said that you want it to mean something, not that it should." His eyebrows drew together. "Do you want to marry me?"

It was only a question, not a real proposal, but Drea felt her stomach drop just the same. Though not in an entirely unpleasant way. The kind of sensation she got right after letting go of the rope swing at the lake, hanging in the air briefly before plunging down into the chilly water.

"Maybe eventually? I don't know. I haven't ruled it out," she replied hesitantly. "Do you?"

"Always have."

Aidan didn't exaggerate. If he said always, he meant always.

"Because I'm the only girl you've hung around," Drea joked, attempting to lighten the mood.

"That's possible." He smiled warmly. "But that's not why."

She swallowed. "Yeah, I know." All at once, everything seemed too intense. She needed some distance to think straight. Lying in bed together was too intimate. She sat up, throwing her legs over the edge of the bed, and moved to get up.

"Drea, where are you going?" Aidan's hand came to rest on her shoulder, gently holding her in place.

"The deliveries still need to be taken care of for the day. It's getting late." It sounded lame, even to her ears.

His voice was unyielding when he spoke. "The deliveries will keep, Drea. We're not finished."

She twisted out of his grip and went to retrieve her clothes. The bloomers she had picked up were snatched out of her hand, and Drea looked up, surprised to find Aidan standing in front of her. He hadn't made a sound.

"We're still friends, aren't we?" It was more of a statement than a question.

"Of course we are." She reached for her drawers, only to have them moved beyond her grasp. "Aidan, stop acting like a child and give me my clothes."

"When we're done talking." His voice brooked no argument. Aidan wasn't a pushover by any means, but he didn't usually assert himself. "Talk to me, Drea. What's wrong?"

"Nothing's wrong." She wished she wore something besides her own skin. "I have a business that needs running."

"No, you're scared, so you're running."

Her chin rose defiantly. "You know me, Aidan Morrison. I don't get scared."

"Then talk to me. What's going on in that head of yours?" His voice had softened.

He'd get the truth out of her eventually. Why keep avoiding the issue? Defeated, she sat heavily on the edge of the bed. Focusing on her toes, she spoke. "We're too close here, and it doesn't feel like such a bad thing. It worries me. That this, us, could maybe work as more than friendship."

"Would that be so terrible?"

Drea didn't answer him and continued studying her toes. Then she wasn't staring at her toes, but Aidan's brown eyes as he crouched down into her field of vision.

"Virgil wouldn't like it, but he'd get over it." Aidan wrapped his hands around hers, thumbs running soothingly over the backs.

"I know," she sighed. "That's part of the problem. He'd see the sense of it eventually. Everyone does. That's where they see this heading, and I can't disagree with them because I can, too. We could get married, and it would work, work real well."

"But?"

"But what? There is no but," she said helplessly. "If there was, I'd have a reason for feeling like this."

"We don't have to get married, Drea. You do know that, right?" He looked at her searchingly.

She looked down at the ring. "I know we don't, but it makes so much sense."

"And when did you start caring about things making sense?"

He was grinning.

And she couldn't fight one of her own in return. "Hey, now."

"Things don't have to change unless you want them to," he said.

"Oh?" she snorted. "They kind of have a way of changing even then."

"That's not what I meant."

"Couldn't help it." She shrugged. "I'd like to actually wear the ring, but I'm not ready for marriage, and that's what everyone is going to think."

"So? Let them. The ring can mean whatever you want it to mean, Drea," he stated firmly. "And if people read something into it that isn't there, you'll set them straight like you always do."

"I will."

"Good. Now let's get to those deliveries." He stood and pulled her up with him.

"Can you do something for me first?" she asked.

"What's that?"

"Kiss me?"

The smile he gave her made Drea's knees go weak as he slowly dipped his head down, capturing her lips with his own. It made her feel warm. It felt right. And that was all it needed to be now.

Chapter Thirteen

Virgil hadn't been able to sit still the entire trip. He spent the last leg of the ride into the station outside Morton's Pointe distracting himself by carrying on an idle conversation with the conductor. He hated to admit it, but he was anxious. Drea and Aidan were meeting him at the station. He wanted to see them but dreaded the reunion at the same time. In truth, he was afraid of how well they had gotten on without him. Did he even have a place with them anymore? And if he didn't—

He forced himself to listen to the conductor's story about his granddaughter's desire for marmalade at all costs.

"And she's barely four. Can you imagine what she'll be like in a few more years?" The man chuckled cheerily.

"Frightening," Virgil chimed in.

"You don't know the half of it. But you will," the conductor said ominously.

He looked at the man, paying real attention for the first time.

"Be starting a family of your own soon, I suspect," his companion went on. "Then you'll understand."

A family? He wasn't even twenty-three yet. How... But no, this was about when that started happening. Regardless of the motivation, Aidan had given Drea the ring, and that was a step in the family direction. Drea had never seemed to hold much interest with the idea, but in a year and a half anything could have happened. People and their ideas could change so quickly.

"You all right there, young fella?" the conductor asked with concern.

"Fine," Virgil replied absently. "I'm fine."

To test how fine he was, the train slowed as it drew near the station. Even going off to war hadn't made him this nervous. Facing almost certain death seemed easier than seeing his best friends again.

The conductor slapped him heartily on the shoulder as the train jerked to a stop. "Cheer up, you're finally home. There's nothing so terrible that friends and family can't make it better."

With that the man went to help the other passengers disembark, leaving Virgil to his own devices. Picking up his rucksack, he decided to bite the bullet and climbed down to the platform.

The air was practically balmy for mid-January. Still cold, but a far cry from the bitter chill it usually held. He had arrived in Chicago during a blizzard, so a break from winter was welcome. Being late afternoon, a few people stood scattered on the platform to greet the arrivals. Young Portney was also there retrieving the daily mail. Spotting Virgil, Young tipped his hat in acknowledgement and continued with his work. Turning to scan the other side of the platform, Virgil caught sight of Drea's unmistakable red hair as she and Aidan came around the corner. He barely had time to drop his bag before Drea let out a squeal of joy and ran full-tilt across the wooden boards to wrap her arms around him in a fierce hug.

"Well, it's good to see you, too." He laughed, swinging her around. He felt foolish for worrying so much.

"Damn, it's good to have you back," she said when he set

her back down, her blue eyes brilliant in her joy.

"If I weren't so happy to see you myself, I might be jealous," Aidan's familiar tenor cut in. "You get an armful of Drea. All I got was a lecture for daring to show up a day early."

"You look good, Aidan," he stated, relieved to see the Aidan he had grown up with and not the broken shell of a man who had been carried out of France.

Aidan shrugged. "Must be Ma's cooking. As hard as Drea works me at the store, it's a wonder there's anything left of me."

"Hey!" Drea backhanded him playfully. "You enjoy every minute of it."

"Being bossed around by you?" he considered. "I suppose it does have its advantages."

It wasn't all that different from the easy camaraderie they'd always had, yet Virgil felt like he was missing out. Paranoia, plain and simple. He was tired and overreacting. Once he got settled back in, caught up on his sleep, had some decent food again, life would get back to normal. He hoped.

His friends filled him in on some of the latest town gossip as the three of them made their way back to the delivery truck. Drea was in the middle of telling him about the new soda shop at Birch's drugstore as she slipped off her mittens to start up the truck, when Virgil caught a flash of silver on her hand. Drea was wearing Great-Gran Morrison's ring. Not on a chain around her neck, but on her goddamned hand. And neither she nor Aidan had thought it worth mentioning to him. Maybe he had a very good reason to be worried about coming home after all.

Somehow, Virgil held his tongue and kept up his end of the small talk as they drove to his uncle's. It was possible they hadn't mentioned anything because there wasn't anything to say. Drea could be wearing the ring just to wear it.

He felt his control slipping bit by bit, attention being drawn more frequently to the ring the closer they got to home. Never in his life had Virgil been more grateful to see his uncle's house. After a good night's sleep, he would be able to look at this a bit more rationally and not blow up at his friends for no reason. He really hoped there was no reason.

While it took considerable effort, he managed not to bolt from the truck the moment it pulled to a stop in the driveway.

"So, you'll come by the store tomorrow?" Drea asked hopefully. "You'd be impressed with what I've done."

Aidan's hand came to rest on his shoulder, getting his attention. "Come by about three-thirty. You'd be doing me an enormous favor."

"Oh no, you're not getting out of waiting on Gladys that easily," Drea chimed in.

Virgil looked between them in confusion. He wasn't even in on the jokes anymore.

"I should have learned after the first time not to make a bet with her," Aidan explained, "but I was hoping to redeem myself."

"Yeah, or you really do like hearing all about Gladys' cats and don't want to own up to it."

Deciding that he didn't care for feeling even more left out, Virgil made his exit. "I better get inside."

"We'll see you tomorrow," Drea called after him as he got out and grabbed his bag.

He was only a few steps toward the house when his uncle came out.

"Virgil, good to see you. Oswald will help you with your things," his uncle informed him briefly before heading to the truck, where Drea had rolled down the window. "Ah, Drea, this saves me a trip."

"What's going on, Raymond?" she asked as if this was perfectly normal.

Virgil knew Uncle Raymond was helping her sell the homestead, which Virgil was less than thrilled about. But to be on a first-name basis with his uncle? Virgil looked to Aidan for insight, and Aidan shook his head, all traces of his good mood gone.

"I received the final papers for the sale this afternoon. If you're able to stop by the bank tomorrow, we can finally finish this," Uncle Raymond told her.

"Sometime after lunch?" she suggested. "Aidan can mind the store."

"Excellent. Until tomorrow, Drea." He grasped her hand and placed a light kiss atop it. He headed back toward the house. "Don't dawdle, Virgil. Oswald's waiting, and Cook is holding dinner."

Virgil waved absentmindedly to his friends and followed his uncle. Things had gotten very strange in Morton's Pointe while he'd been gone. Very strange indeed.

‘’

After his uncle made a few polite inquiries into his trip home, dinner was a silent affair. Virgil waited until dessert before broaching the subject that had bugged him since Drea and Aidan dropped him off.

"What game are you playing, Uncle Raymond?"

The man's eyebrow quirked up as he set aside his spoon. "Game, Virgil?"

"With Drea."

"Drea came to me for help in selling the homestead. It's not a game, Virgil; it's business."

Virgil snorted. "Uncle, it's never just business with you. You could never stand my hanging around her and Aidan. But now you're helping her as if it's the most natural thing in the world? I'm out of the loop, not stupid."

"If you're worried about someone taking your girl, Virgil, I'm not the one you should be looking to," Uncle Raymond stated with a smirk.

"Drea's my friend, not my girl. There's a difference," Virgil replied evenly, feeling the cold metal of the spoon handle dig into his hand.

"Like Aidan Morrison is your *friend*?"

Was it possible the man knew what he and Aidan had been up to? Yes. Raymond Craig hadn't gotten as far as he had in life without finding out what other people had thought carefully hidden.

Before Virgil could speak, his uncle continued, "They've become quite an item, those two. The Morrison boy has been working at the store with Drea since he got back and has been known to stay quite late. Though, from what I've seen, that store only needs one person to run it."

"Friends help one another out, Uncle. That's what they do."

"Yes, I suppose they do." He picked up his spoon and resumed his dessert. To him, the conversation was over. "Oh, before I forget, you'll be starting at the bank the first of the month. I trust you'll find some way to keep yourself occupied until then. Unless you had other plans?"

Virgil kept his peace, not trusting himself to speak. He'd just gotten home, and he was supposed to know what he was going to do? He didn't want to go work for his uncle. But until his trust came due in a couple years at twenty-five, he was beholden to his uncle's wishes unless he found some other means of supporting himself. University was an option, but he had no desire to subject himself to more schooling. That was Aidan's thing.

Aidan. Something was going on between he and Drea. Or not. Virgil was tired, very out of sorts and talking to his uncle hadn't helped matters. He'd stake his life on the fact that Uncle Raymond was up to something with Drea.

He had a lot of catching up to do, but he wouldn't be doing any of it tonight. Right now, he didn't have the energy. It could all wait until he slept and had time to get settled.

Chapter Fourteen

Virgil returned from putting his motorcycle through the paces to find Aidan leaning against the doorway leading into the carriage house, waiting as if he had all the time in the world.

"Afternoon, Virgil."

Virgil brought the bike to a stop, dismounted and walked it the rest of the way in. Aidan was angry, but you wouldn't know it to look at him. He was the only person Virgil had ever met that could act less angry the angrier he got. Virgil had good reason to believe his friend upset. He'd been avoiding the store and Drea and Aidan in the three days since he had gotten back.

After parking the bike in its corner spot, he acknowledged, "Aidan."

Aidan followed, reclining against one of the posts while Virgil set about wiping the motorcycle down. "You must be pretty busy out here. Can't think of anything else that would keep you from visiting your friends."

Knowing full well Aidan was going to see through him, Virgil didn't look up when he replied, "It takes awhile to get settled back in, you know."

"It does," Aidan acknowledged. "But it also makes a convenient excuse to avoid people."

"I'm not avoiding."

"The ring doesn't mean what you might think." Aidan cut straight to the matter at hand.

Virgil did look at him.

"Do you really think I can't tell by now when something's bothering you?" Aidan asked, his tone still conversational. "Hell, even Drea noticed once we were on the way back to town, realized she was wearing the ring and put two and two together. I'm surprised you didn't blow up then and there. You did when I first gave it to her."

"Well, I didn't much feel like starting a fight the moment I got home. And I hoped I was being paranoid."

"Jealous, you mean." Aidan flashed him a quick grin. "And rightly so. I've had Drea to myself for almost a year. No telling, is there?"

"I wish you didn't know me so well." He cleaned his hands on the rag and tossed it aside, walking over to join Aidan against the wall. "So, if the ring doesn't mean what I might think, what does it mean?"

"Friendship, I guess."

"You're not planning anything?"

The corner of Aidan's mouth quirked up wryly. "Oh, there's a number of things I'm planning, but marriage isn't one of them." When he spoke again, his voice was as casual as it had been the whole time. "We've been together, Drea and I. A few times now."

"Oh," Virgil said, stunned. Not because his two friends were fucking, he really should have figured as much, but more at the easy way Aidan told him. Like he was recounting the weather. Virgil found his voice. "So there is something going on between you two."

"Something, yeah. But if there's a name for it, I haven't

found it. I never could figure out what you and I had going, either." He shrugged. "And the worst part is that every time I'm with Drea, I can't help but think of you. How different you both are. How similar."

Virgil said quietly, "It's incredible, though, isn't it?"

Aidan nodded. "Incredible doesn't even begin to describe it."

They stood there, lost in their own thoughts.

"It's all going to go to hell, isn't it?" Aidan mused with a hint of resignation. "How can it not? I was expecting it to this afternoon when I came here. I was expecting you to get upset, angry. Not this."

"Not this what? Me managing to carry on a civil discussion?" Virgil inquired with a note of humor. "Maybe the war mellowed me."

That earned him a derisive snort from Aidan. "You? Mellow?"

"Stranger things have happened. Look at automobiles. Horseless carriages used to be a joke."

"You're comparing yourself to the evolution of transportation?" Aidan's eyes danced in amusement.

Virgil responded the only way he could. He slugged his friend hard in the upper arm. "You never used to be so sarcastic."

Aidan rubbed his arm, but grinned. "Makes up for you mellowing out."

"Remember how well trying to take over my role as asshole worked out for you before?"

"Doesn't suit me, does it?"

"You have too big of a heart for it to be anything but temporary."

"And you don't?" Aidan fixed him with a discerning look.

115

"You've got a hell of a temper, my friend, but deep down, even for you being an asshole is temporary."

"So, I'm a big softy under the gruff exterior?" Virgil joked, not wanting to admit outright how dead-on Aidan was. It was easier to be a jerk than compassionate. Could be why they were such good friends. Aidan was everything Virgil wouldn't let himself be.

"Well, I don't know as I'd go that far," Aidan laughed.

God, it was good to be back. Almost felt like he'd never left, that the whole past year and a half hadn't happened. But when he was in France, Morton's Pointe hadn't seemed real, either.

"You all right?"

"Mostly." Virgil's good mood evaporated. "It's weird. Now that I'm back, I feel like this is all there ever was. But when I was overseas, the war was all there ever was. I thought it would take longer to readjust."

"It does, and it doesn't," Aidan informed him thoughtfully. "You fall back into routine fairly quickly. But every so often something will come up that reminds you of the war. Something as simple as the fall of shadow in the afternoon or the godforsaken mud, even the smell of fresh baked bread coming out of Foster's Bakery. But maybe that's only me. I was the one who went crazy."

Aidan's voice only held a trace of bitterness, which was good in Virgil's opinion.

"You've been doing all right?" Aidan's letters had been full of plenty of detail, just none of it about himself.

Aidan shrugged, leaning back to stare at the rafters. "A few nightmares here and there, but I left most of the bad stuff in the hospital. Or I've done a really good job of repressing, and it's going to bite me in the ass one of these days. Maybe that's why I keep myself so busy. Drea thinks I work at the store to help

116

her, when it's really for me. Especially since Da looked at me like I was nuts when I offered to help out around the farm."

"You hate farm work. You always have."

"I know. But work is work. I hardly ever spend time alone anymore, even when reading. I like having someone else nearby. I crave company like I used to crave solitude. Maybe I am repressing."

"Maybe it's the best way to get through the day," Virgil suggested. "It's good not to get too wrapped up in your own head, regardless of what you've gone through."

He saw Aidan's lips twitch with amusement.

"What?"

"Virgil Craig has grown insightful. I don't think I can handle that on top of the mellowing."

"You're really set on the title of chief asshole, aren't you?"

"I might be at that."

Frowning, Virgil said, "Speaking of assholes, why's my uncle suddenly all friendly with Drea?"

A dark look crossed Aidan's face. "He was helping her sell the homestead."

"I know that, but why? Out of the kindness of his heart?"

"That's what our girl believes." Aidan sounded bored, as if he'd been over this too many times to invest much emotion in it.

"Drea's not stupid." Virgil pushed off the wall and paced in front of Aidan. "And she knows Uncle Raymond."

"Well, she's decided that she was wrong all these years."

"Because he treated her decently?"

Aidan threw up his hands in a "beats me" gesture.

Virgil went on. "The man's only nice to people he wants

something from."

"Do you think he'll cheat her?" Aidan stood straighter, showing more interest in the topic.

Virgil shook his head. "From what I've seen, he's good that way. Not the most honest, and he'll make a more handsome profit than he should, but Drea will still fare well in the end."

"Do you think your uncle might be in this for Drea?" Aidan asked, his tone indicating that was exactly what he thought.

"No, that's crazy." But it really wasn't. The way Uncle Raymond held himself around Drea the other day, the tone of his voice...it differed little from how he behaved when he chatted up the girls at Madam Violet's. Virgil slammed his fist against a nearby beam, the impact echoing through him. "Fuck."

"That's more like the Virgil I know and love." Aidan's hand came to rest on Virgil's shoulder. "That's what you think, isn't it?"

"Not think, know," Virgil said tightly. "Goddamn it. The way he's always talked down about her, I never thought. But he's always had an eye for the redheads. Madam Violet herself and at least three or four of the other girls. I don't think I've ever seen him with anything but."

He started to throw his fist again, but Aidan caught his wrist.

"It won't do us any good if you break your hand over it," Aidan said calmly. "It would piss you off even more, and you're angry enough."

Virgil growled in response but didn't try to break away.

"Glad I'm not reading too much into things, then," Aidan added. "I've never thought of myself as the jealous type, even when I *was* jealous."

"That's why you're friends with me," Virgil pointed out. "You can be calm and rational while I handle the anger and jealousy."

"It's worked out pretty well so far."

Feeling less homicidal, Virgil smiled. "I'm assuming you tried talking to Drea?"

"Actually," Aidan hesitated, "I haven't broached the subject with her since shortly after I got back. As you can imagine, I got nowhere. But with it being your uncle and all, she might listen to you."

Virgil laughed. "Want to bet?"

"Seeing as I'd lose, no," Aidan replied with a grin. "But you'll still talk to her, right?"

"Yeah, I'll talk to her." Virgil then said, with a hint of flirtation, "You going to make it worth my while?"

"Friendship isn't enough anymore?" Aidan's fingers tightened slightly around Virgil's wrist.

"Friendship has always been enough." Virgil caught and held Aidan's gaze. "But it doesn't mean I don't want more."

Aidan's brown eyes grew darker. "More is nice," he agreed, voice slightly hoarse. He pulled Virgil forward, mouth attacking with a hunger that Virgil readily welcomed.

He groaned, pulling Aidan tighter against himself. It had been too long. Too long since he had felt the solid planes of Aidan's body beneath his hands. Too long since he had tasted Aidan's mouth, so eager and pliant against his own. Too long since he had been able to lose himself in one of his oldest friends.

"Drea's not expecting you back at the store anytime soon, is she?" Virgil shoved Aidan's jacket off.

He could feel Aidan smile against his neck, fingers tugging

at the tails of his shirt. "Not until tomorrow. We both thought it would take me some time to explain what's going on to you."

"It's a real shame I turned out to be so reasonable." Virgil worked his hands beneath Aidan's suspenders, enjoying the feel of Aidan's chest beneath the soft material of his dress shirt. "You've become a regular dandy, Morrison." He pushed the suspenders over Aidan's shoulders.

"Well, I can't dress like a farm hand when working at the store, can I?" Aidan worked at the fly of Virgil's jeans. "And I'd be careful about who you call a dandy. Wait until you start working at the bank."

Virgil's groan was only partly due to annoyance at the reminder; Aidan's hand had found its way into Virgil's jeans, fingers wrapping with familiarity around his cock. "God, that's good," he breathed when Aidan began to stroke him in a steady, slow rhythm.

Aidan chuckled. "Been awhile for you, has it?"

"You have no idea." He unfastened Aidan's trousers. Following Armistice, there'd barely been time to have a quick flirt with one of the French village girls. And he hadn't done much before the war had ended, either. The girls weren't half as skilled as Madam Violet's, and he'd gone off sex not long after Aidan had been sent home. The casual fucks left him feeling cheap when all was said and done. The constant fawning and transparent desperation of the girls made him ill. The actual fighting and what he saw on the marches were enough to depress him without adding to things.

"You all right, Virgil?" Aidan pulled back to look at him.

"Yeah. It has been awhile."

Aidan's left hand came up to cup his cheek. "I told you the war creeps up on you at unexpected times."

"Inconvenient more like."

"There never *is* a convenient time for it. Believe me."

"Distract me," he said to Aidan.

"I can manage that." His right hand tightened briefly around Virgil's cock. "Any particular distraction you had in mind?"

Virgil tugged Aidan close and whispered against his ear, "Fuck me."

Aidan made a low, indefinable sound. "Yeah?" He sounded like he hadn't dared hope for it again.

Virgil looked at Aidan straight on. "Please, Aidan. I need to feel you right now."

"Got anything here we can use?"

"I don't know about you, but I'm not all that keen on motor oil."

"That's just wrong, Virgil."

"You asked."

Aidan sighed, but the effect was offset by the smile tugging at his lips. "I'm betting you don't have any of that stuff from Madam Violet lying around, do you?"

"We used it up that day we enlisted, remember?" God, that had been a day. Almost as intense and heedless as any time during their first spring together.

"And you never picked up more?" Aidan chastised teasingly.

Virgil grinned. "Sorry, but I've been busy."

"Now what kind of excuse is that?"

"One you can't argue with."

"Good point," Aidan conceded and kissed Virgil hard and hungrily. "We'll make do with what we have."

"Spit it is." Virgil grabbed Aidan's left hand and guided the first two fingers into his mouth. He took his time, tongue thoroughly reacquainting itself with each digit. He took pride in the effect his simple attentions had on Aidan, jaw slightly slack, eyes dark and breath increasingly rapid. Yeah, he'd missed this.

He released Aidan, drawing back by gradual degrees. "That should be a good start," he said lightly as he turned to face the wall, shoving his jeans down as he did so.

He felt Aidan press close behind him, fingers slipping knowingly between his cheeks and circling the hole hidden there. "You're a tease, Virgil."

Virgil's laugh turned into a low groan as one of Aidan's fingers began to work inside. Voice strained, he countered, "A tease would get you all worked up and walk away. I'm not going anywhere."

"No, you most definitely are not," Aidan chuckled.

Aidan added a second finger to the first, cutting off Virgil's retort. One finger had been fine, but Virgil found the second took a little longer to get used to than he remembered.

"You all right?"

Virgil nodded, bracing himself against the wall and forcing himself to relax. It wasn't as bad as the first time, at least. And the burning sensation of being stretched began to fade into the dull throb of anticipation. Aidan, who had always been good at reading him, started to move his fingers in slow, easy strokes, gradually getting him ready.

"God," Virgil sighed, "I forgot how good you were at this."

"It's all those secondhand lessons from Madam Violet." He could hear the amusement in Aidan's voice.

"Madam Violet's good, but I don't think you can give her all the credit."

"That's probably the best compliment you ever gave me,

Virgil," Aidan replied with a quiet laugh as he withdrew his fingers. Before Virgil could complain at the loss, he heard Aidan spit and soon felt Aidan's cock nudging at his opening. "You ready?"

"More than," Virgil breathed.

He felt only the faintest sensation of burning as Aidan pushed his way inside. It felt too good after so long to care about any discomfort.

Aidan leaned heavily against Virgil's back. "I missed you, Virgil," he murmured.

Virgil reached blindly for Aidan's right hand, holding it briefly and guiding it forward to wrap around his cock. "This last year has been hell, and that's not including the war. The worst of it was not knowing whether I'd have a place here when I got back. And not only because you and Drea might have moved on without me. But that maybe I couldn't come home again."

"Afraid the war had changed you too much?" Aidan suggested, remaining motionless behind and around him.

"Yeah."

"You'll be surprised when you discover how much and how little it has."

If anyone would know, Aidan would. Nevertheless, Virgil found little comfort in his friend's words. "I'm glad you've reached a definitive answer on the subject."

"Sorry, Virgil, that's about as good as it gets."

Virgil wasn't used to Aidan being sarcastic, but he wasn't in the mood to dwell on it. What he was in the mood for was distraction. And Aidan was perfectly situated to distract the hell out of him.

"Aidan?"

"What?"

"Can we talk about this later?"

"Are you telling me to shut up and fuck you, Virgil?" Aidan laughed.

"And here you used to be the upstanding one," Virgil tsked.

In response, Aidan's hips moved back, cock withdrawing almost completely before thrusting back inside. Virgil didn't think he'd ever felt anything so wonderful. Aidan repeated the motion, adding his hand into the mix, moving in counterpoint along Virgil's cock. Virgil groaned.

Teeth nipped lightly at his ear before Aidan said in a voice too low to be borne, "Are you sure you wouldn't rather talk?"

"Oh, I'm very sure," he replied steadily.

"Good, because neither would I." And Aidan proceeded to drive any other thought out of Virgil's mind.

Chapter Fifteen

Drea had been on edge since Aidan left that afternoon to go talk to Virgil. Predictably, the store had been quieter than normal, with no deliveries that afternoon and only Gladys' daily visit an hour before closing. It left her too much time to think. She really hoped Aidan would be foolish enough to trek back into town that evening and fill her in on what went on, but it wasn't likely. If only she could have found some logical reason for him to take the delivery truck.

The familiar roar of Virgil's motorcycle interrupted her preparations for dinner. It couldn't be all that bad if he was stopping by himself.

Running down the stairs, Drea opened the door and greeted him with a bright grin. "Well, it's about damned time."

The corner of his mouth quirked up. "Haven't been waiting on me, have you?"

"I was beginning to think I'd dreamt you coming back. Three days and not a word?" she chastised, her tone light.

Virgil shrugged, running a hand through his hair and looking past her. "I've been settling in. And there is a bit more distance between Uncle Raymond's and town than Uncle Raymond's and your old place, you know."

"So you're just lazy then, not avoiding me?" She felt uneasy. He seemed amiable enough, but faint tension ran through him. And why wouldn't he look at her?

"Why would I be avoiding you? I wouldn't be here if I was avoiding you," he pointed out.

Something was going on. "What's wrong, Virgil?"

He did look at her then, gray eyes dark, almost angry. His voice held no trace of that anger when he spoke. "I've been away for a while, Drea. There are a lot of changes to get used to."

Virgil didn't do quiet anger. When he was mad, he let you know it. He didn't hold himself back. Hell, most of the time, he flew off the handle quicker than she did. If Aidan had explained everything, Virgil shouldn't be angry. Unless... Had Aidan been stupid enough to tell Virgil they'd been sleeping together? While they weren't exactly keeping it a secret from Virgil, you didn't spring that on one of your friends. Especially one as volatile as Virgil.

"Can I come in, Drea? It's a little cold out, being winter and all."

She shivered. "Sure. Right." She moved to the side so he could enter. "The stairs are to the left."

"I know the way." He moved past her.

Relocking the backdoor, she followed him upstairs.

She found him examining the few knick-knacks she kept on the mantle. He picked up a worn photograph of the three of them from the Harvest Festival a half-dozen years back. All bright smiles and young, so very young. They hardly resembled themselves much in it now. Kids. Not all that long ago, and yet it might as well have been forever. Back before war and sex and rings were ever a concern.

"It used to be so simple, didn't it?" Virgil asked as if reading her thoughts. He carefully set the picture back on the mantle and faced her. "We need to talk, Drea."

126

God, he sounded so adult. When had that happened? Absent-mindedly almost, she twisted the ring on her right hand. She had switched it from her left hand after the first time she tried it on to avoid any possible misunderstanding. But people often saw what they would regardless.

His lips twitched. "Don't worry, this isn't about the ring. If I hadn't figured it out for myself, Aidan explained it pretty clearly so there wouldn't be any confusion this time around."

Drea blushed, remembering the day he had fucked her in the barn, angry and quick and... She wished Aidan would try that, just once. She didn't mind the slow, worshipful caresses, but she wanted more sometimes. Like how she missed having a no-holds-barred shouting match with Virgil. She craved the fight, where your blood ran hot and you held nothing back. But that wasn't Aidan's style.

She shook her head. This was not the time to compare the boys. Or ever. She was with Aidan now. Well, sort of. It wasn't right to bring someone else into the mix, even if Virgil was always there in the background.

"What is this about?" She disliked the uncertainty in her voice.

"You and Uncle Raymond." His voice had an edge to it.

"What about Raymond and me? He helped me sell the homestead," she replied easily. "He's president of the bank and one of the most successful businessmen in town. Why shouldn't I ask him for help?"

"It's Uncle Raymond, Drea." As if that were all the explanation needed.

"I know you two don't get along, Virgil, but he's not that bad. Maybe it's because I'm not some ragtag kid running around with his nephew anymore."

"I'd say it's definitely because you're not a kid anymore." He

127

ran his hand back and forth through his hair. "My uncle's not a kind man. He doesn't do things out of the goodness of his heart."

"Of course he doesn't. He's a businessman," she said, hurt that he thought her so naïve. "And I know that Raymond wouldn't have tried to find a good buyer for me if he didn't stand to make a good profit. That's why I went to him. I didn't only want the house off my hands, I wanted to make some decent money to set aside. For the future, maybe for the store. Actually, he had this idea that, while risky, would probably be my best shot of branching out. Raymond thinks that a speakeasy would be a—"

"*Don't* call him that," Virgil cut her off with a sharp hiss. Before she could speak, though, he forged ahead. "You're out of your league and you don't even realize it."

"Out of my league? Because he's the big bad businessman and I'm the poor clueless girl attempting to run her own store?" Had Virgil forgotten who she was?

"Doing business with Uncle Raymond. I thought you were a smart girl, but as you're mixed up with him now, I'm thinking not."

She blinked, stunned. "Why wouldn't I go to him if I wanted to guarantee myself the best sale possible for the house? Raymond's made a success of his life doing that and more."

Virgil grew angrier. Both his hands clamped tightly on her upper arms as if to shake her. "*Stop* calling him that, Drea."

"It's his name, Virgil. I'm not a child, I don't need to call him Mr. Craig anymore," she said derisively. "Besides, he asked me to call him 'Raymond'."

"He's using you, Drea."

"It's business. We're using each other to make a profit."

His grip tightened, fingers digging in. If he kept this up, she would have bruises. Not that she minded; she'd given him worse on a few occasions. Aidan would have a fit, though.

In all honesty, she had missed having someone who could match her temper. It felt good to get this upset.

"Uncle Raymond's not interested in profit with you," Virgil stated tonelessly.

Drea couldn't help but laugh. "And what is he interested in? Me?" The look he gave her told her that was exactly what he thought. She shook her head. "What have you always said about Raymond and his little trips to Grand Rapids? That he goes to Madam Violet and her girls because they're far enough away not to touch any part of his life up here. He can have all the fun he wants without any of the consequences."

"You're forgetting," Virgil said, voice quiet as he leaned in close, "Uncle Raymond gets bored and likes to mix things up. You're something new to play with."

"Gee, then it's good you came back to save me, isn't it?" she spat. "Are you really worried for me? Or upset that I can actually get along with your uncle? Or maybe"—she felt her lips curl—"you feel threatened? Are you jealous of your uncle, Virgil?"

"Because he's got you well and thoroughly conned? Hardly," he growled. "The only person I have any cause to be jealous of is Aidan, but at least that makes sense. What you have going with my uncle doesn't. You know what he's capable of, Drea, and yet you're playing right into his hand."

"It's not like that," she protested. "If he were seducing me, I'd know."

"Would you really? You've been playing with boys, you have no idea what men are capable of."

Drea stood up straight and said triumphantly, "Well, seeing

129

as you are one of those *boys*, I hardly think you're the one to enlighten me."

Virgil's eyes flashed at the challenge. "You don't think so?" His voice went so low that she felt more than heard it. He pulled her flush against him and moved his lips near her ear. "Those trips to Grand Rapids weren't only about sowing my oats. A Craig doesn't only know what to do with a woman; he also knows how to get her."

His mouth captured hers, laying a hungry claim that left her no option of resisting. She was aware of every line of his body, so solid against her.

Breaking away, he looked at her, eyes dark and sparking with danger. "I didn't do things proper the first time, and I know Aidan doesn't have a clue. I think it's time I remedied that."

Before she could protest, his mouth was on hers again as he scooped her into his arms and moved with quick strides to her bedroom. She knew she should stop this somehow, keep him from gaining the upper hand, but with her body on fire, she really couldn't think of a reason why that mattered. Instead, she kissed him back with as much passion as he had initially kissed her.

Virgil broke the kiss and stared at her when they stopped by the bed. "You have no idea how easily a man can play your body to make you helpless and willing to give him whatever he wants."

It took some effort, but Drea spoke evenly when he set her back on her unsteady feet. "I don't remember you ever being so full of yourself, Virgil. You can be charming, I'll grant you that. But I doubt you can be *that* charming. You're too impatient."

He spun her quickly in his arms so her back was against his chest. His right hand rested firm against her stomach, holding her in place while the left wandered up to lightly tease one of her breasts. Drea could feel his breath, heavy but controlled as it danced across her ear. "I can drive you mad with how patient I can be."

"Can you really?" Her voice was too breathy to give the words any real strength. Oh no, he wasn't going to win that easy. He could use every trick Madam Violet and her girls had taught him, but Drea would prove him wrong. Somehow. "Do your worst, Virgil Craig," she challenged, voice stronger until his lips began to ghost along the sensitive skin of her neck just below her ear.

"Do you know how my uncle would start?" he murmured against her neck, the words as much a caress as what he was doing. "He would tell you how beautiful you are, all passion and fire, capable of so much if guided by the right hands. You've played with boys for so long, Drea, he would say, but you've outgrown them. It's time for you to know what men can do."

Virgil's hand abandoned her breast and worked open the buttons that held her top closed. Slipping beneath the material he began to explore again unhindered.

Swallowing hard, Drea spoke and tried to add a bit of venom to her words. "You may want to rethink your plan of attack, Virgil. This really isn't all that different from that time in the barn."

She felt his head pull away. "Isn't it?" he inquired with a curious note in his voice. "Maybe not yet, but it will be."

The bottom of Drea's shirt was tugged free from her waistband before hands moved upward and drew it down from her shoulders to land by her feet. Virgil's lips whispered softly against her neck again as he unfastened the closures of her skirt. A gentle nudge from him and gravity did the rest of the work to leave one less layer between them.

"Bit by bit, layer by layer, he would expose you," Virgil said, lips moving from her neck to her left shoulder. His fingers pushed the strap of her chemise down, leaving his path unhindered. "He would undress you properly, leave you naked and bare. Before, I didn't bother to take the time. It's amazing what you can do while still mostly dressed. But I wish I had, Drea. It's even more amazing what you can do when completely undressed." He moved over to repeat the same attention to her other shoulder. "You and Aidan have taken your time, though, haven't you?"

Drea stiffened at the mention of Aidan. "Don't bring him into this."

"Why not? Isn't he as much a part of this as either of us?"

"Virgil, don't," she said more firmly and tried to move away.

She didn't get far before he pulled her back snug against his body, his grip viselike as he restrained her. She felt his lips dance across her ear when he spoke, his voice a dangerous, low sound. "I know you think about me when you're with him." He didn't give her a chance to respond, his right hand trailing down her abdomen to run lightly along the waistband of her drawers, untying and pushing them to the floor. "It makes you feel guilty. But you shouldn't, Drea. The three of us have been a part of each other's lives for too long, you can't separate from that. And there's the fact that I had you first."

Virgil was right. She could forget him for a little while with Aidan, get caught up in the moment and sensation, but inevitably Virgil crept into her thoughts. It felt like a betrayal to think of one while with the other, but like Virgil said, it had been the three of them for so long that when it was only two of them, things weren't the same. And now that she was with Virgil and not distracted from her thoughts, Drea couldn't help but think about how hurt Aidan would be to find out she was with Virgil again.

"And now that you're with me, you're thinking about him, aren't you?" he murmured knowingly, his fingers teasing along the borderline of hair leading to her sex, going no farther and tracing back and forth.

She couldn't do this. Not right now. Maybe not ever again. No, definitely not. She couldn't do this to Aidan. She wouldn't let Virgil do this to Aidan. "Stop, Virgil, please stop," she managed at last, her voice choked. "We can't do this."

He spun her to face him, forcing her chin up to look at him. His gray eyes were stormy. "Yes, we can," he informed her. "We can, and we are."

Drea tried to resist him at first when his mouth claimed hers, tried to deny him entrance, but he eventually won through, quieting her protests as he enticed the needs of her body forward. Soon she pressed into him, demanding more.

Virgil guided her back onto the bed, never breaking the kiss as he eased her to the mattress and moved above her, still fully dressed.

"Do you trust me?" He gazed down at her.

"I...always," she replied. And she did. "Why? What are you—"

He shook his head. "If you trust me, trust me." He flashed her a quick smile before backing down her body, moving closer toward—

"Virgil?" She was perplexed.

Drea had her answer as Virgil settled himself between her legs, and nudged them farther apart, opening her up to him. His breath danced hotly over moist, sensitive flesh. Suddenly, his mouth was on her, lips placing a gentle kiss before his tongue darted out and ran between the folds hidden there.

She sat up with the intensity of the unexpected contact.

Her first instinct was to move away, quickly. But Virgil's hand came up to rest firm but gentle against her hip.

"Drea, lay back and trust me," he said soothingly. "You'll like this, I promise."

Maybe, maybe not. But it seemed strange as hell to see him down between her legs. "You sure about that?" He was the one with the experience and all, yet... "Did you pick this up in France? Because you never mentioned it before."

"What fun would there be if I told you everything, Drea? It's good to have a few surprises in life." Virgil grinned up at her. "And yes, I am very sure about this. Trust me."

"All right, Virgil." She willed herself to relax. He seemed perfectly comfortable with this situation. "As long as you know what you're doing."

He chuckled. "You have no idea."

Drea sighed and lay back, figuring this would be a lot easier if she wasn't watching him.

"Good girl," she heard him murmur before his mouth descended onto her pussy once more.

He wasn't in any hurry, taking his time to memorize every fold and contour. It was different than probing fingers. Gentler and far more intimate. Drea shivered as his tongue ran over her clit. She'd swear she felt him smile, but then he licked again and again and again and she really couldn't think beyond the sensation he elicited. He kept on until she thought she would lose her mind. He finally gave her a brief respite, backing off to seek out new territory. She felt the tip of his tongue tease at her opening, circling around and around before pushing in, shallow at first, but gradually deeper. With sex and the beforehand fumblings, she always felt stretched and full. This almost felt better. It felt good right off, no getting used to anything.

Her hips arched off the bed, following his tongue as it

moved upward. Virgil's movements became quicker, more intense, pulling Drea right along, building her higher until she couldn't take it anymore and came shuddering with a hoarse cry.

Blissful moments passed as she lay there, boneless and floating in contentment. She slowly became aware of her surroundings again, blinking her eyes open to find Virgil beside her, head propped up on his right hand as he watched her. He looked extremely pleased with himself, which, she supposed, he had every right to be.

"That was amazing," she said at last.

Her admission pleased him greatly. "It really was."

She smacked him ineffectually across the chest. "Watch it." Curious, she asked, "So did you pick that up in France, or is that more of Madam Violet's careful instruction?"

"Madam Violet."

"She's a good woman."

Virgil laughed. "Madam Violet does know what she's about, I suspect."

"You need to take me down to Grand Rapids one of these days. I'd love to meet her." Virgil's eyebrows shot up. "I mean it."

"I can't take you to a whorehouse, Drea."

"Why not? It's not like there's anyone around to know or care." She grinned. "I bet Daddy'd roll over in his grave. But I've done a lot of things that have probably made Daddy roll over already—selling the homestead, sleeping around..."

Virgil sobered somewhat at her words. "You aren't sleeping around."

"Well, I've been with you, I've been with Aidan, I'm here with you again. That's sleeping around."

He was in motion before she realized it, bracing an arm on either side of her as he peered down. Only then did Drea realize how very naked she was while Virgil was still fully dressed. She felt even more vulnerable than earlier when he had been down between her legs.

"Me and Aidan, that's not sleeping around."

He was more serious than she'd ever seen him before.

"What do you mean? If I'm not with either one or the other of you, that's sleeping around."

He shook his head. "Sleeping around is when you're in it solely for the thrill and physical pleasure of it all. It's different when you care about the people you're with." He sounded like he was trying to convince himself as well as her.

Vulnerability replaced by a sense of unease, she reached a hand up to cradle the side of his cheek. "What's going on, Virgil?"

"Nothing." He looked off to the side before focusing back on her.

"Virgil."

"It's nothing, Drea."

She could press the issue, but Virgil wouldn't give up his secrets until he was good and ready. "All right." She ran her fingers lightly through his hair. "You know, it really is good to have you back, Virgil. I missed you."

"Missed you, too, Drea. You have no idea." He dipped his head down to kiss her lightly. There was a faint, salty taste that she hadn't caught before. It was her, and that fact didn't bother her.

"Oh, I don't know about that." She curled her hand around the back of Virgil's neck to draw him closer and tasted herself on him again. She found it immensely satisfying. "I have a pretty good idea."

Virgil was finally home. Worry could wait.

Chapter Sixteen

Drea's inability to meet Aidan's eyes when he arrived at the store that morning would have been a dead giveaway, if Virgil hadn't forewarned him about what was likely to occur. It was further supported by the blush rising to color her cheeks when he asked how their conversation went.

"He didn't convince me that I'm wrong about trusting Raymond, if that's what you mean." She took great care to make certain the cans on the shelf were aligned just so.

"I didn't think he would, but I figured it wouldn't hurt for him to try."

Her shoulders tensed. "Believe it or not, I am capable of looking out for myself. I managed quite well when you two ran off. Before that even. And while I might not be as worldly as Virgil or you, I have a pretty good idea when I'm being played with."

Aidan sighed. He'd expected as much. Walking up behind her, he said soothingly, "We know you can look out for yourself, Drea. But sometimes you can be too close to something and need a bit of outside perspective to see clearly."

She whirled on him and jabbed a finger into the center of his chest. "Raymond Craig is not seducing me. It's business. That's it. Why you and Virgil can't get that through your thick skulls, God only knows."

He held up his hands in surrender. "All right, point made." She'd never believe them until Virgil's uncle showed his true colors. Solid, irrefutable proof was often the only thing that got through to her.

"Somehow, I doubt that," she muttered, brushing past him.

"You get up on the wrong side of the bed this morning?" he called after her.

"How's that any business of yours?"

Her words evoked an unexpected flare of jealousy. Knowing something and being confronted with the reality of it were two very different things. To make matters even more awkward, heavy footfalls descended the back stairs preceding Virgil's arrival into the store proper. He drew up short when he saw Aidan was there.

"You weren't kidding about getting here first thing in the morning, were you?" Virgil attempted lightly.

"Bad habit of farm life. Always up with the sun whether I want to be or not." Aidan tried to keep his tone as light.

"You were supposed to be gone by now, Virgil," Drea reprimanded.

Virgil shrugged. "It's not like Aidan didn't know I'd be here."

"He knew you were coming over last night, *not* that you'd be here in the morning," she nearly growled. But Virgil's placid expression seemed to clue her in, and Aidan found himself the focus of Drea's ire once again. "You knew, didn't you? The way the evening might go?"

Nothing would be helped by lying. She'd only get angrier. "Isn't that better than keeping it from me?"

She considered him through narrowed eyes. "You're not kidding, are you?" When he shook his head, Drea's face flushed even more, fists clenching by her side. "Jesus Christ, Aidan, what'd the two of you do, work out a schedule beforehand as to who can fuck me when?"

Virgil came forward and stood next to him. "It's not like that, Drea."

"Then what's it like, Virgil?" she asked through clenched teeth.

"Last time I checked, we were all still friends here. And friends don't keep secrets from each other and go behind each other's back, do they?"

Aidan groaned. Oh yeah, that wasn't setting them up for a nasty fall. He could only imagine Drea's reaction to finding out about what he and Virgil had been up to the last few years. And yesterday in the barn. Well done, Virgil, well done. It was only a matter of time before she flung that comment right back at him. *If* she ever spoke to either of them again.

Drea's mouth thinned into a fine line. "This is different. And I don't much care for the idea of the two of you comparing notes on me."

Aidan attempted to intervene. "Drea, we don't—"

"Spare me, Aidan, please," she silenced him icily. "If I didn't know better, the way the two of you go on about each other when one of you is in bed with me, I'd be liable to think you had something going on."

His heart stopped. Literally stopped before resuming a hard, steady beat that echoed through his body, ticking off every second until it all fell apart. Fuck.

Virgil forced a laugh. "You didn't get up on the wrong side of the bed this morning, you got up on the crazy side. Me and him? Honestly, Drea, you lose all the sense that you were born with?"

The smart thing to do was deny it. It was the only option

that allowed any of them to walk away from this in one piece. But it still hurt Aidan to hear Virgil dismiss their relationship so easily.

Drea had her mouth open for a sharp retort, but Aidan didn't have the stomach to handle her and Virgil's sniping over this.

"I have to get out of here." He cut between them toward the front door.

"Aidan, where the hell do you think you're going?" Drea called.

Pausing at the door, he looked back. "I can't do this. You two can play this how you always do, shouting at each other and everything else. But I'm not going to stand here and keep you in check, like I always do. Maybe it's time you two didn't have me holding you back."

Virgil started forward. "This involves all of us, Aidan. You can't walk out."

"If I don't walk out, I won't be standing on the sidelines. And I doubt what I am likely to say will help matters," he said, tone flat, even and heavy with meaning for Virgil's benefit.

He exited the shop, slamming the door behind him. After clearing the town limits, he ran every mile home in an attempt to lose himself in the pain of unaccustomed exertion.

He arrived home exhausted, out of breath and in plenty of pain, but the thoughts were still there. Virgil wouldn't tell Drea, which left it up to Aidan to tell her. And he had to tell her, because he was going to have no peace with himself until everything was on the table. Virgil would hate him for it. And Drea was liable to hate them both. But that was the way of it.

"Aidan, is that you?" his ma called from the front porch. "What are you doing back so soon?"

"Drea didn't need me today," he replied, glad that he wasn't telling his ma an outright lie.

"Good, you can make yourself useful here. The dining chairs need mending. Your father's never going to take a hand to it if he can help himself, and the other boys are worse than he is about fixing things." Minor carpentry was the one chore he'd never completely loathed.

He headed for the house. "Thanks, Ma. I'd be happy to do that."

"Happy?" She frowned up at him as he passed. Then the frown was replaced by concern. "You feeling all right, Aidan?"

"Yeah, nothing a bit of hard work won't help." He forced a smile and went to gather the chairs.

♋

That was how Virgil found him, in his father's makeshift workshop shortly after lunchtime. Busy working on the lathe, he didn't notice he had company until Virgil stood right in front of him.

"Didn't expect to see you so soon. Drea scare you off finally?"

Virgil frowned. "Fight kind of went out of us with your big, dramatic exit. Tough act to follow."

"Less dramatic than if I'd stuck around."

Virgil's eyes narrowed discerningly. "You would have told her."

Aidan looked at him, unblinking. "And about damned time. This has gone on for too long behind her back. It's only going to get worse the longer we keep it from her."

"Maybe. But today was definitely not the day to do it."

"Why do you think I left? You might be able to lie about us to her face, but I sure as hell can't." He bent back to the chair leg he was working on.

There was silence before Virgil asked, "Are you mad at me for staying over with her last night?"

"I said I was fine yesterday when you told me, and I'm still fine with it today."

"Then what are you pissed at me about?"

"I'm not pissed at you, Virgil." He sanded the lathed pine faster.

"Seems like you are."

Aidan's hand stilled as he got a hold of himself. Setting the sandpaper down, he walked away from the lathe, past Virgil to stare out through the window at the back fields. "I'm tired. And not exactly thrilled about things going to hell now. I wasn't counting on there being problems this soon."

He felt Virgil come up behind him. "Problems are all we're going to have if you keep walking away and don't talk to Drea and me."

While Aidan had been hurt earlier, he was pissed now. His jaw clenched tightly as he kept himself in check. "Fine one you are. I'm the only one of the three of us who ever does talk. You and Drea avoid or scream. That's the point I'm at right now. And I've told you, if I start acting like you two, there won't be anything left." He paused. "Believe me, Virgil, if I got in on it now, that's not an exaggeration. We're all better off with me avoiding."

"Is that your way of telling me to get the hell out of here and give you some space?" Virgil stood right behind Aidan, close enough that his breath stirred the light hairs on Aidan's neck.

"Which seems to be something you have no intention of doing," Aidan said with a short, bitter laugh. "The best thing for all of us is space. Before one of us does or says something that makes this worse."

Virgil's hand came to rest heavily on his shoulder. "Look at me, Aidan."

"Just go, Virgil. Please."

The hand became insistent, tugging on his shoulder to turn him. But he resisted. Or tried to. Eventually, he had to concede and face Virgil.

"You're upset because I could lie to Drea about us, aren't you?" Virgil asked quietly.

"It's the only way you could respond." Aidan looked over Virgil's shoulder. "It hurt, though. I expected it, but it still hurt."

The hand on his shoulder moved to his neck, fingers wrapping around gently and thumb running lightly along his jaw. Aidan savored the contact. Virgil's denial hurt because it fell from his lips so easily, despite the fact that he seemed to be as affected by things between them as Aidan was.

When Virgil spoke, his voice was quiet and sincere. "I'm sorry, Aidan."

He shrugged. "Couldn't be helped. Your back was up, and, really, how else could you have responded without giving anything away?"

"I'm still sorry."

"I know," he sighed, looking at Virgil. His gray eyes were dark and troubled. "We knew it was going to be a fine mess. Doesn't make the reality any more fun, though."

Virgil nodded. "What makes it worse is that I'm not about to give up either of you to keep this friendship of ours from crumbling. But I've always been a selfish bastard that way."

Aidan found Virgil's words strangely reassuring.

He continued. "Besides, I can't go back to being just friends with you or Drea. Not because it would be awkward, but because after having more, I can't settle for less."

Aidan brought his hand up to cover Virgil's. "I could settle for less again, but"—he softened his words with a wry smile—"I really don't want to."

"That leaves us with a big dilemma, doesn't it?"

Reaching forward with his free hand, Aidan grasped the front of Virgil's jacket and pulled him closer. "One that isn't going to get resolved anytime soon," he said, his voice low as they stood there, pressed flush against one another. "I came out here so I wouldn't have to think about our troubles for a while, but I find I'm not all that distracted at present. Think you can help with that?"

The grin was genuine this time. "I may have an idea or two that might do the trick."

Virgil lightly captured Aidan's lips with his own. Aidan felt no small amount of relief at the touch and granted Virgil immediate entrance. The kiss was almost gentle, lacking the frenetic need and urgency that usually colored their times together. A nice change of pace after yesterday and a welcome balm for the morning.

He pulled Virgil along as he backed up to the wall, savoring the easy exploration of their mouths. Virgil pressed into him, a solid, steady presence, hips rocking enough to elicit a slight friction along Aidan's hardening cock and leaving no doubt as to Virgil's response.

Aidan groaned in protest when Virgil broke the kiss. A satisfied smirk settled on Virgil's lips as his hands moved to the waistband of Aidan's pants.

His voice was husky when he spoke. "Do you have any idea how much I enjoy having this effect on you?"

"I think I have a vague idea," Aidan replied with a chuckle as Virgil undid his fly in short order and pushed the material far enough out of his way to have unhindered access to Aidan's cock.

"Vague idea?" The fingers of his right hand grazed lightly along Aidan's shaft. "I know it's better than vague." With a quick kiss, he dropped to his knees, pumping Aidan's cock once, twice before his mouth wrapped around the head and followed his hand down.

"Christ, Virgil," he breathed, the hot, slick heat of Virgil's mouth overwhelming his senses. The first time Virgil had done this to him Aidan thought he might lose his mind. There had been no awkward fumblings as when Aidan tried those first few times, leaving him to wonder how thorough an education Madam Violet and her girls had given Virgil. Could have been natural talent. In any event, it was good, and only got better over time as Virgil learned which spots were the most sensitive and when to bring his tongue into play. The only downside was that Aidan felt like a rank amateur, though Virgil never seemed to mind.

Aidan let his head rest against the barn wall, eyes drifting closed and fingers threading through Virgil's hair as he lost himself. He needed this. Beat hard work for forgetting his problems any day, even if this was related to the problems he wanted to forget.

He felt the tension in his body build as his release neared. As if sensing it, Virgil's efforts redoubled, working until Aidan came with a sharp cry, shooting deep into Virgil's welcoming mouth.

Sated, Aidan leaned against the wall while Virgil brought

him down. He always enjoyed the moment after he came, however long or short it ended up being. Pure contentment. There was no world or worries, only blissful oblivion. It never lasted long enough.

He opened his eyes with a reluctant sigh as Virgil started to pull away, only to nearly choke on the escaping air as he saw that they weren't alone. Drea stood in the doorway of the workshop.

Her jaw hung slack, blue eyes brilliant and staring. Before he could move or speak, she regained possession of her faculties, shook her head, mouthed a silent "no", turned and fled.

Virgil muttered, "Fuck," as they watched her disappear.

Aidan pulled his pants up, fastened them and set after Drea before Virgil even had a chance to get to his feet. He reached the truck as she was starting to open the door and threw his entire body against it to slam it closed.

"Get out of my way, Aidan," she growled, tugging on the door handle.

"You're not leaving. Not until Virgil and I get a chance to explain."

Virgil arrived, out of breath.

"Explain? What's there to explain? It was pretty obvious what was going on." Her voice was cold and even.

"Drea, please." Virgil reached for her, but she quickly eluded him.

She crossed her arms, blue eyes snapping defiantly. "Please what, Virgil? I don't think I owe either of you anything."

She was too calm. Oh, she was angry, there was no denying that. And hurt. But she wasn't in a rage like she normally would be. Drea's controlled anger didn't bode well.

Her unforgiving gaze settled on him. "How long?"

"Drea, there's no reason to—"

She cut Virgil off. "Aidan, tell me how long this has been going on. I deserve to know that much."

He was the one who wanted to get it all out in the open, wasn't he?

"Aidan." Impatient, commanding.

No point in delaying the inevitable. "Remember that day you told us you were going to the festival with Bill?"

"As if either of you would let me forget," she spat. "And what does that have to do with—oh." Her brow furrowed. Aidan had a sneaking suspicion she was calculating, which she confirmed when she said in a very small voice, "Three years?"

Virgil exhaled, and Aidan could only nod.

"*Three* years. And not a single word," she said more to herself than to them, staring at her feet. "Nothing at all." She looked up, eyes shining. "You never trusted me."

Virgil took a step toward her, but when she put out a hand to keep him back, he held his ground. "It's not like that, Drea. It kind of got away from us."

She laughed a humorless sound that was almost a sob. "Three years is not something that kind of got away from you. A handful of times, maybe. But *this* is something you deliberately kept from me."

"We're sorry, Drea. You don't know how much," Aidan attempted.

"Apparently not sorry enough to tell me." She seemed about to say more, then threw up her hands. "I'm done. All I know is that I'm getting the hell out of here and neither of you are going to stop me."

Aidan could see that Virgil was going to argue further, but

there was no point. She wouldn't listen, and she had every right not to. To Virgil he said quietly, "Leave her be." Then he backed away from the truck, leaving Drea's exit clear.

Virgil looked between the two of them and moved out of the way with a muttered, "Fine."

As they stood there in the snow and bitter January cold, Drea speeding down the road, Aidan wondered if there was a point when it was best to keep on lying. Lying wasn't fair or right, but lying wouldn't leave a big gaping hole where one of the most important people in your life used to be. Still, you couldn't do it forever; the truth always came out in the end.

Sighing, he turned to Virgil. "We need to go after her. Not right away," he said as Virgil opened his mouth to comment. "But soon. Give her maybe an hour or so to get home and settle in a bit. Because I have a feeling if we don't keep talking to her, regardless of whether or not she listens, there will be no saving this."

"She's not going to listen," Virgil agreed. With forced humor he added, "At least we have numbers on our side. Two of us versus one of her. That's something, isn't it?"

Yeah, it was something. But Aidan doubted it was going to be much in their favor.

Chapter Seventeen

Drea sat by the side of the road in the no man's land midway between the Morrison place and Morton's Pointe. The delivery truck had gotten a flat and, to make matters worse, she hadn't replaced the spare tire after the flat she took the previous summer. Afternoon was starting to fade, and she needed to start walking toward town soon. A flat tire on top of catching her best friends fooling around with each other... She breathed deeply, focusing on the biting January cold. She would *not* cry.

Aidan and Virgil being together made perfect sense, now that she thought about it. Why else would they be okay with each other having a go with her? If they had told her way back what was going on, she would have accepted it, eventually. Two men having relations wasn't the accepted way of doing things, but it did happen—there'd been stories about Hezekiah Smith and his "cousin" Davey for as long as she could remember, not to mention her ex-Uncle Thomas who her father refused to acknowledge. Hez and Davey were always nice when they came in to the store and seemed like everyone else.

Aidan and Virgil had deliberately kept this from her. Left her to stumble across them and discover it for herself. They'd lied to her and been lying to her for three years. That cut her deep. It was like they didn't care about her at all. Drea wondered if they'd fucked her out of guilt. Or maybe she was a stand-in for when the other wasn't there.

"Fuck them both." She sniffed back the tears creeping up on her. Rubbing at her eyes, she tried to pull herself together. They didn't deserve her tears.

The sound of a car rolling to a stop over exposed gravel startled her back to the world. No one hardly ever used this road. Which meant that Aidan and Virgil *had* come after her. The fools.

She got to her feet, intent on walking into town. They could follow. But she would not talk to them.

"Drea?" The voice that called after her belonged to neither Aidan nor Virgil. It was rich and deep with a note of concern that many people would have found uncharacteristic. She turned to find Raymond Craig walking toward her. "Are you all right?" he asked.

The question undid her. Her attempted reply came out as a harsh sob. Raymond's arms wrapped around her as the full force of her emotions finally overwhelmed her.

How long she stood crying against Raymond's solid chest, Drea couldn't say, but when she pulled herself together enough to look up, dusk had settled about them.

"I'm not crying because I got a flat." She didn't want him to think her a silly girl upset over nothing.

He smiled warmly. "You never struck me as the type to let the small things get to you." He glanced up at the sky and, following his gaze, Drea realized that snow was starting to fall with the fading light. Looking back at her, he suggested, "What do you say to going some place to warm up? Then we'll see about getting you sorted."

"That'd be nice." She let him lead her across the road to his car.

Twenty minutes later, Drea stood in front of a roaring fire, wrapped in a heavy mink blanket, thanks to Raymond's butler's quick efficiency. Osgood? Oswald! That was it. Not the friendliest of people she had ever met, but a person didn't hire a butler from one of London's most prestigious services for companionship. While Raymond wasn't the *only* person in Morton's Pointe with a butler and assorted household staff, especially amongst the summer tourists, he was the only one who had his direct from London, England. A number of the townsfolk, including his nephew, thought it pretentious. But it suited him, in Drea's opinion. Besides, Raymond was the one footing the bill, he should be able to have whomever he wanted.

The liquid rattle of ice on glass gave Drea a start. With a grateful look, she reached out to take the glass from him, sniffing tentatively at the contents, then smiling a bit wider. "I suspect you keep this around purely for medicinal purposes?"

He chuckled. "Purely."

She took a sip. The liquor had been watered some, but it still burned as it traveled down her throat. The heat felt good. It would feel a whole lot better if the liquor weren't so weak. She finished off the drink and held the glass out to him. "Can you please not water it down this time?"

Gray eyes danced in amusement as Raymond inclined his head. "My kind of girl," he murmured, taking the glass from her.

Drea felt her cheeks. Perhaps any other time the words would have troubled her, but right now flattery in any form was more than welcome.

"Thank you for this," she said when he returned. "I really don't think I could stand being home alone just yet."

"I'm always grateful for the company. You're more than welcome to come by any time, even when you don't have a flat tire." Sincerity underlay his light tone.

It was a far cry from the glowering, dark looks she and Aidan used to get from Raymond whenever they came by to see Virgil. Aidan and Virgil. She could feel the tears threatening to start again. No. She was done crying over them.

Drea considered the glass in her hand, amber liquid winking in the firelight. There wasn't even ice this time. Good. Steeling herself, she finished off the liquid in two swallows. Her eyes smarted and her throat ached, but, God, it was good.

The appreciative light was even more apparent in Raymond's gaze now as he watched her.

"I might regret that in a few minutes, but right now that's exactly what I needed," she stated as the alcohol settled in her stomach.

"Do you think you're ready to talk about what happened yet?" He gently guided her toward the couch to sit.

Drea sighed as she settled against the leather, toying with the edges of the blanket. "Frankly, I'd like to forget it completely, but I have a feeling that's impossible." She debated the wisdom of confiding in Raymond, what with Virgil being his nephew and all. But who else did she have? "I saw something today that I wasn't supposed to see. But it wasn't what I saw so much as the fact that that's how I found out."

"You walked in on Virgil and Aidan, didn't you?" His tone gave nothing away.

How could he possibly—actually, she shouldn't be surprised. She had a feeling there was precious little Raymond Craig didn't know.

He smiled without humor. "I won't say I was exactly pleased when I found out, but believe it or not, Drea, relations between two men are not all that uncommon."

Hesitantly, she asked, "How long ago did you find out?"

"A couple springs ago."

Nothing like being the last to know. She slumped against the back of the couch. "I never thought you'd be all right with something like that."

Raymond shrugged. "Let's say that I believe everyone is entitled to do what they wish in their private life."

"Such as your biannual visits to Madam Violet's." She slapped a hand over her mouth. "Shit, I didn't mean...I'm sorry, Raymond."

His warm chuckle put her at ease. "Yes, such as occasional visits to Madam Violet's." There was a fond note to his voice when he continued. "Madam Violet is quite a remarkable woman. You would like her, Drea. She's no-nonsense with an excellent business sense."

"Virgil's always spoken highly of her." Then Drea admitted, "Always wished I could meet her. And not for curiosity's sake, mind you."

"Though I'm certain curiosity plays a role." He winked.

"Some." She grinned in spite of her embarrassment.

He took the empty glass from her hand and set it behind them, returning to clasp her hand lightly in his larger one. "If you ever get down to Grand Rapids, you should pay her a visit."

Drea imagined herself walking up and knocking on the front door of an elaborate brothel, asking if she might pay a call to Madam Violet. She giggled. When she realized what a fool she was being and risked a glance at Raymond, she only giggled harder. Breathless, she apologized. "I—I don't know what's wrong with me."

"It's the whiskey settling in. Give it a moment; it'll pass."

She sighed in relief when she felt in control again. "I am

going to be so glad when this day is over. Though it is ending better than it began."

"I'm glad I could help."

"I don't know what I would have done if you hadn't happened along. Well, no, that's not true," she amended. "The cold would have gotten to me, and I would have dragged myself into town." Drea sat up with a start. "The truck! Damn. I suppose I can get Ed Allen to give me a ride out when I buy a new tire from him tomorrow. Make that two tires, since I won't risk going without a spare again."

"There's another option, you know," Raymond gently cut into her ramble.

She blinked at him, curious.

"I have a perfectly good spare lying around and gathering dust in the carriage house. After dinner, I'll drive you back to the delivery truck, and we can switch your flat out. Then you can stop by Ed's when it's convenient to get yourself that other tire," he finished as if it was the most reasonable solution.

Which it really was. But the only response she could come up with was, "Dinner?"

His lips curled up in amusement. The man ought to smile more, it looked good on him.

"I can't send you home on an empty stomach, can I? Contrary to popular opinion, I do possess a few manners." He held up a hand when she started to protest. "No, you're not putting me or any of my staff out. And I doubt you've eaten at all today, am I right?"

Come to think of it, she hadn't had much of anything since lunchtime the previous day. She never got around to dinner last night and only had a couple slices of bread on the way down to open the store that morning. Her stomach grumbled to further support her realization. She was starving. "Dinner would be really welcome. Thank you."

cs

Dinner was a fairly silent affair as Drea spent the bulk of it eating everything in sight. Raymond didn't seem bothered by her near lack of manners as he sat back, watching her with quiet amusement. Having a cook had its advantages; she couldn't remember the last time she'd had such a good meal.

Afterward, they retrieved the spare tire from the carriage house and drove back to where her truck was stranded. She was fully prepared to change the tire herself, but Raymond wouldn't hear of it and bent to the task himself.

Raymond Craig doing manual labor, it was...it was funny. She couldn't help laughing.

"What is it this time, Drea?" he asked lightly, still focused on attaching the tire.

"This. You helping me. Everything."

"It's not what I'm known for, I'll be the first to admit."

She crouched next to him, placing her hand on his arm. "I really do appreciate all you've done for me, Raymond. It means a lot."

He finished tightening the last bolt and set the tire iron aside, then clasped her hand in his as he stood, pulling her back to her feet.

"It's been my pleasure." His voice was soothing and low. "You've become a remarkable woman, Drea. Anyone who can't see that is a fool."

Let it not be said that Raymond Craig didn't know how to flatter a girl. Drea was warmed by his words. Or perhaps it was the contentment of an excellent meal and a considerable amount of alcohol.

"And I would be a fool for not doing this." He closed the distance between them and bent down to capture her lips with his. The kiss was light and fleeting, almost chaste, but it enticed Drea forward, seeking more. Raymond was happy to oblige, if the smile she felt was any indication. His left hand came up to cradle the base of her skull and the kiss turned from chaste to questing as he gained gradual entrance to her mouth. It progressed slowly until she found herself breathless when he pulled back. She had a sneaking suspicion that if not for the hold Raymond had on her neck and waist, she might not be so steady on her feet.

Blinking up at him a bit dazed, she licked her lips before managing a whispered, "Damn."

"I have been wanting to do that for a very long time," he admitted.

Aidan and Virgil had been right all along, she realized. But the reality didn't bother her. Was it so horrible that Raymond Craig wanted her and had likely only been winning her trust over the last year to get to this point? It was good to be wanted. Now more than ever.

"Isn't this a little dangerous for you?" She toyed with the front of his coat. "Getting involved with a local girl?"

"Reputation isn't always reality, Drea," he replied with a touch of amusement. "It's not dangerous so much as I haven't found the right person nearby until now."

He had the moves and knew exactly what to say. It was very possible he would drop her after he got her into his bed, or not long after. But again, would that be so terrible?

Last night Virgil had tried to show her what seduction was, how his uncle would win her over. She had seen a new world of possibilities. And she had enjoyed it very, very much. Even if it had all been an act on Virgil's part, covering up what he and Aidan had going on behind her back. She pushed the thoughts away. She didn't want to feel hurt and betrayed, had managed to forget during her time with Raymond. Why couldn't she forget a little longer and find out if Virgil had been nothing more than a pale imitation? His words from the previous night came back to her, and she couldn't help but take them as her own.

"I've been with boys, Raymond. Show me what I've been missing." Her voice came out a lower pitch than she'd been expecting, but judging by the hungry look on Raymond's face, it was very good.

When he kissed her again, gone was the subtle, slow ease of the first. No, this was all-consuming and full of heat and passion, and there was a skill to it that couldn't be denied. Driven but controlled. The small part of her brain that was still coherent sighed with relief when he spun them and pinned her against the side of the truck. The kiss left her weak and begging for—no—demanding more. Maybe she would regret this in the morning, but right now losing herself with Raymond Craig seemed like the best idea in the world.

Until the approaching roar of a motorcycle engine cut through the pleasant haze of lust to bring reality crashing back. She broke away from Raymond to stare at the approaching headlight. Virgil wasn't the only person in Morton's Pointe to own a motorcycle, but Drea had a feeling it wasn't likely to be anyone else.

And it wasn't.

Virgil barely took enough time to shut off the bike before he was off and charging at his uncle. Virgil's punch knocked Raymond back onto the road.

"You son of a bitch. Couldn't wait to move in on her, could you?" he seethed, bending down to haul Raymond to his feet by the lapels of his coat. His fist cocked back to hit Raymond again.

That spurred Drea into action, and she lunged for Virgil's arm, holding him back. "Don't you dare strike him again, Virgil!"

"Take your hands off me, Drea," he said with cold anger.

Before she could respond, Raymond's right fist connected with Virgil's jaw, sending both Virgil and Drea stumbling back.

Raymond flexed his hand. "You had better think long and hard before you try to take me in a fight, Virgil. There will be consequences you aren't ready to deal with." His voice was calm and controlled, much the same as if he were conducting a very serious business transaction. Raymond wore subtle danger about him, the kind that made people sit up and pay very close attention. If they were smart. This was the man who had intimidated her for much of her youth, who demanded respect. And while it was still intimidating, a part of Drea found it extremely attractive. Much like when Virgil put his foot down and managed to keep his anger reined in. God, they had more in common than similar physical traits. It shouldn't have come as such a surprise, and yet...

Virgil stood his ground but didn't move to strike again. When he spoke, his anger was still very evident, as was the effort to hold himself back. "Drea's *my* friend, Uncle, *mine.* You do not get to do this to her."

"And what exactly is it that I'm doing to her, Virgil? Showing her some respect, a bit of compassion? Jesus, what a monster that makes me." Sarcasm laced Raymond's voice. "As for being Drea's friend, you'll have to ask her, but, personally, fucking that Morrison boy behind her back for the last three years doesn't strike me as being a paragon of friendship."

"'That Morrison boy.' You never could call Aidan by name,

could you?" Then Virgil's tone grew calculating when he continued. "But Drea used to be 'Jeb Samuels' brat' until she grew attractive enough to bed. You never did much care for the company I kept."

Christ, she'd rather they slugged it out instead of sniping at each other.

Drea stepped between them. "Enough already." They looked at her. "I don't need this tonight. You two can settle this without me here." She gave Raymond a small smile. "I had a lovely evening and wish it hadn't come to such an abrupt end." Then to Virgil, she said, "And I'd rather not see you anytime in the very near future."

She started the truck up and was ready to pull away when there was a rap on her window. It was Virgil.

Rolling the window down, she stated curtly, "What?"

"Aidan's at the store."

Fuck.

"We came looking for you. Because while you might not give a shit about us, we still care what happens to you," he said. "And seeing that you weren't there, Aidan stayed behind in case you showed up, and I came back out to find you. So, if you can bear to see me once more this evening, I'll follow you in and take Aidan home."

"Do what you want, Virgil," she sighed, longing for bed and for the day to finally end. Too much had happened, and she didn't know what to make of any of it. Maybe if she had a few minutes to herself, she could. But in a place as small as Morton's Pointe, that was next to impossible. Especially when the people she was trying to get away from kept coming after her.

Chapter Eighteen

If Aidan weren't waiting at the store, Virgil would have let Drea drive off, while he stayed behind to settle things with his uncle once and for all. Or attempted to. Judging by the way his jaw still ached, Virgil wagered that, despite the sedentary lifestyle his uncle seemed to lead, the man was more than capable of holding his own in a fight.

Virgil opened up the gas on the motorcycle, closing in on the red taillights that had pulled far ahead of him. The icy sting of the air as it whipped by distracted him from the thoughts roiling through his head. But as his face grew numb to the cold, the image of Drea in his uncle's arms flared up as fresh as ever.

Was it possible that she had been aware of Uncle Raymond's intentions all along, maybe even welcomed them? Virgil shook his head and hunched lower over the bike. Any other time she would have pushed the man away, he was certain. She was hurting from catching him and Aidan, so she decided to hurt Virgil right back. She couldn't possibly be attracted to a man who was only a few years younger than her own father had been, could she? No. Especially not when the man was his uncle. It wasn't right.

He ground his teeth as he and Drea neared town. No way in hell Raymond was getting anywhere near her.

As they pulled to a stop behind the store, Aidan ran out to greet them. Drea was already out of the truck and heading to the store before Virgil could even think of dismounting his bike.

Drea yelled at Aidan, "See, I'm fine. In one piece. Go home, Aidan." She made as if to brush past him, hell-bent on getting inside the store and locking both of them out, but Aidan reached out and hauled her back.

"We're not leaving until you give us a chance to explain," he said calmly.

Virgil thought leaving was probably the smartest option, especially after what he'd seen. He wasn't much in the mood for explanation and civil discussion. But maybe that's what they needed. A no-holds-barred argument where everyone laid everything out. Hell, even Aidan. It might have been better for them all if Aidan had stuck around that morning instead of walking out.

Drea was trying to twist away as he neared them, so he grabbed hold of her other arm. "There is a lot that needs to be discussed before any of us goes home for the night," he informed her coolly.

She looked at him, mouth set in a fine line. "You're both wasting your time. You really are."

Virgil decided to bring Aidan up to speed. "You know how we've been warning Drea about Uncle Raymond? Well, seems that's what she wanted from him all along. Caught them by the side of the road just now." He had to swallow back some of his anger before continuing. "But what I can't figure out is whether things were getting started or if they were finishing up."

Drea's gaze settled on him, full of loathing, disgust and disbelief at what he'd accused her of.

"She was with Raymond?" Aidan's voice was so very quiet.

"What's that matter to either of you?" Drea spat. "Neither of you want me, but no one else can have me? Bullshit." She finally managed to wrench free from their grip and turned on them. "For all you talk down about Raymond and what a villain he is, at least he's honest. He's never pretended to be what he wasn't or hide what he's done from me. So for as much of a bastard as Raymond Craig might be, he's a better person than either of you."

With that, she headed inside, slamming and locking the door behind her.

Virgil stood there, stunned. She was right. He hated to admit it, but she was right. Outside of turning up the charm, he doubted his uncle had ever flat-out lied to her. Hell, Uncle Raymond would have loved Drea calling him on every misdeed and questionable thing Virgil had told her about over the years.

"No, this is not how this ends. Raymond Craig is not the better man," Aidan growled, suddenly in motion. Virgil watched in dismay as Aidan bent down, retrieved a brick from beside the stoop and proceeded to smash it through the bottom pane of the window, the breaking glass shattering the silence of the winter night.

Virgil reached for him. "Aidan, what in the hell—"

Aidan shook Virgil off and cleared the glass out of the way and reached in to unlock the door. He wrenched the door open and stormed inside, leaving Virgil gaping after him.

He could hear Drea's voice from the stairwell when he followed Aidan inside. "You and your goddamned temper, Virgil Craig. Breaking my window. What's ne—" The words died as she discovered Aidan was the guilty party.

Virgil reached them in time to see Drea retreating up, and Aidan steadily advancing on her. She was no longer angry. She was frightened. And so was Virgil. This wasn't Aidan's style.

"None of us are running anymore, you got that?" Aidan's

measured words resonated in the narrow space. "Virgil and I are coming upstairs, and the three of us are going to sit down and settle this once and for all."

Aidan forged up the stairs, leaving Drea no choice but to get out of his way or be run down.

As Virgil followed mutely, he realized he had never seen Aidan truly angry before. And after tonight, he hoped he would never see it again. Drea looked at Virgil helplessly as he joined her at the top of the stairs to watch Aidan prowl around the room. He stopped and studied them from the other side.

The left corner of his mouth curled up in what would have been amusement in other circumstances. "This might be the first time I've had your undivided attention." Drea looked ready to interrupt him, but he held up his hand. "And I aim to keep it for a bit longer until you and Virgil have heard everything I have to say. So you might as well make yourselves comfortable."

"Aidan, what in the hell—"

"Let him say his piece," Virgil cut her off. "He's more than earned it." There was a determined set to Aidan's jaw that said he'd fight for the right to speak. "Come on, Drea." Virgil pulled her toward the couch. They settled on either end and waited.

Aidan ran a hand through his loose hair, a glimpse of nervousness showing through his outward façade of control. "Right then."

And this was why he didn't act rashly. Aidan hated getting into something without having at least a vague idea of how it would go. He wasn't good at doing things on the fly. But there wouldn't be a better time than now to break out of routine. No more agonizing.

He focused on Drea. "I want to know straight out, how far have things gone between you and Raymond?"

Her anger flared again, but she held herself back. Mostly. "If I said he had me six ways to Sunday by the time Virgil found us, could you handle that?"

"I wouldn't care much for it, but there'd be no changing the truth of it, would there?" he replied tonelessly.

She nodded, seemingly satisfied. "Don't think I'm not going to hold you to that, Aidan Morrison." Then she took a deep breath and let it out. When she spoke again, her voice was softer. "No, Raymond and I haven't fucked. The kissing Virgil saw was the extent, aside from dinner and an understanding ear when I needed one. But if Virgil hadn't come along, it's very likely I would have gone back to Raymond's tonight."

"You told Uncle Raymond about us?" Virgil growled, turning on her, something akin to murder radiating off of him.

Drea remained unfazed. "He guessed; I didn't have to *tell* him much."

It went a long way to explaining why Raymond had grown colder toward him as the years went on. He wasn't only Virgil's poor farm boy friend, but his lover as well. Frankly, he was surprised that cold was all Raymond was toward him.

"He believes that everyone is entitled to do what they like in their personal life," Drea said with a hint of admiration.

Virgil's face twisted in disgust. "He said it because it was what you wanted to hear."

Her eyes narrowed into vivid blue slits. "What would you know about it? Have you ever given your uncle half a chance? No, you had your mind set from the day you moved here. If you'd quit being so damned stubborn for two seconds, you'd see that he doesn't deserve all your criticism."

"One afternoon and you're suddenly the expert?" Virgil scoffed. "The man has never cared about anyone but himself."

Before Aidan could stop himself, he intervened. "If that was true, he'd have packed you off to an orphanage and you know it, Virgil."

Arms crossed over his chest, Virgil spat back, "Thanks a lot, Aidan. Take her side *again*. Would it kill you, just once, to support me?"

The anger that had simmered down since they'd gotten upstairs rose in Aidan once more. "I'd take your side if you could ever come up with a position that held any merit. You get angry, Virgil, and all sense goes out the window."

"Sense." Virgil stood and crossed the room to stand toe-to-toe with him. "I really don't think you want to go there, Aidan. For the model of reason, you didn't show much of it in France, did you? Where was your logic and sensibility then?"

Aidan didn't have time to see red before his fist connected with Virgil's jaw, sending him stumbling back. Anger followed action, and it took every bit of restraint Aidan possessed not to strike Virgil again.

Instead of more sharp words goading him on, pressing the point as Virgil was wont to do, he looked up at Aidan as he worked his jaw, utterly stunned.

"I don't think I ever deserved to get hit more in my life," Virgil said. "That was beyond cruel, Aidan. I'm sorry."

He could see that Virgil was genuinely taken aback, truly sorry. But it had hurt. "Fuck you, Virgil. There is no sorry for a comment like that."

Virgil opened his mouth to speak, but Drea beat him to it. "It was uncalled for, but you know he didn't mean it, Aidan. And for that, yes, there can be sorry." She moved to stand by Virgil's side. "I've got letters you never saw that prove how much he doesn't mean that."

If it was possible, Virgil looked more shocked by Drea's

defense than anything else that had been said or done that evening. Aidan was surprised, too. When Drea became the coolheaded one in their group, they were in trouble.

Then to prove that this wasn't completely removed from normal, she whacked Virgil solidly on his arm. "Would it kill you to think before you opened your mouth? Life would be a hell of a lot easier for you and everyone else."

Despite the anger he still felt, Aidan couldn't help the small grin that tugged at his lips.

"What?" Drea looked at him curiously.

"It's good to know that some things don't change."

"Can't help reflex," she replied, the barest hint of amusement in her voice.

Rubbing his arm, Virgil chimed in, "Well, your reflexes hurt like hell."

She flashed him a smug look. "Wouldn't get your attention otherwise, would it?"

"No, I guess not."

An uncomfortable silence settled around them. Anger abated somewhat, but it still hung heavy around them.

Aidan sighed, at a complete loss. "What happened to us?"

Drea's face hardened. "What happened to *us* is that *you* have been lying to me for the past three years."

"Right. Because we weren't having any problems before you found us out," Virgil stated tersely.

"That was completely different," she shot back.

"Was it?" Aidan interjected. "We're still trying to treat each other the same way we have been for the nearly fourteen years we've known each other, but we can't. Things have changed, have been changing for a while, and we've ignored it. *That* is why we're in this mess. We can't act like friends is all we are

167

when this has gone way past friendship."

"What are we supposed to do, then?" Drea asked expectantly. Virgil's stance echoed the sentiment. If Aidan was going to tell them the problem, they wanted him to have the solution as well.

He didn't have one. Unable to look at them anymore, he walked over to the window and stared into the black night. No way could this end without someone getting hurt. They could attempt to go their separate ways, for all the good it would do them. Distance wasn't possible in Morton's Pointe. That left trying to be *just* friends again, because it wasn't right to keep things going between two of them and leave the third out in the cold. At least, he couldn't do that, couldn't choose between them. But maybe they could. Drea and Virgil wanted to be with each other. Aidan had always thought things would lead that way, considering how they fought and flirted over the years. He knew better than to think he was only a stand-in for one of his friends with the other, and yet... Watching them play off one another, a person would have to be blind and stupid not to see the potential there.

Maybe that *was* the solution. He could remove himself from the equation, leave them no choice. If it was the only way to keep them in his life, he could handle it. Besides, what he and Virgil had going had been wrong from the start, good as it felt when they were together and as much as he craved it when they were apart. And being with Drea had been better and more than he ever hoped for. He could be content with what he'd had with each of them.

No, he couldn't. He gripped the windowsill as if his life depended on it.

"Aidan?" It was Drea's voice, so he assumed that the light hand on his shoulder belonged to her. "What's going on in that head of yours, Aidan?"

He could lie, keep his mouth shut, put their feelings before his like he always did. But he was sick of coming second or even third with himself. Staring at his hands, knuckles turning white, he said, "I thought maybe I could step back and let you and Virgil be together. But I can't."

"Aidan." This time it was Virgil, his voice low and insistent. "Aidan, look at us."

Realizing he had little choice, he turned to face them. "What is it, Virgil?"

"You don't want to give either of us up. What's so horrible about that?"

"The world doesn't work like that."

"Doesn't it?" Virgil's tone was thoughtful.

Aidan shook his head. "Aside from the fact that I'm sure Drea wants nothing to do with either of us. It doesn't work that way."

"Hold on." Drea stepped forward. "I'm pissed as hell that you two lied to me about what's been going on. But I understand why you did it. That's not something I can hate you forever for. For a while, yeah, maybe. But not enough to want to throw you both over."

"It's always been the three of us," Virgil continued. "Why should that change?"

Drea's eyes went wide when the implications of what Virgil was saying finally hit her. "Wait, you mean...oh."

"And like I said," Aidan cut in, "that's not the way the world works."

"It does happen, though," Virgil put forth.

"That might be, but it can't last."

"Why not?" Drea asked. They looked at her. "I honestly
169

want to know why it can't."

A number of examples from Aidan's reading over the years came to mind. Triangles were always doomed. Someone inevitably got left out in the cold regardless of how good the intentions were in the beginning. Then again, in those cases, the attraction didn't extend between all parties. He shook his head. If he thought things were bad now, they would only get worse if the three of them went that route.

Finally, he answered her. "It never lasts because three always becomes a crowd in the end."

"So you won't even consider it," Virgil said, disappointment clear in every word.

"We'd end up hating each other."

He caught Drea's skeptical look. "And we won't if we keep on like we are?" she stated.

He sagged back against the wall. No matter what they did or didn't do, it wouldn't end well. If they walked away now, at least they'd cut their losses. His heart ached at the thought. He didn't want to lose them.

"I think it's our best option," Drea said decidedly. "Leave it to Virgil to come up with the craziest solution."

"You really mean that, don't you?" Aidan studied her. Eventually, she nodded. He looked to Virgil. "And you meant it."

"Yeah, I did. But I've always been a selfish bastard," he added lightly.

Aidan cracked a smile. "You're right about that."

Any other day, Drea would have laughed the idea off as completely absurd. But in a day filled with absurdity, it made the most sense. Considering she felt as if a herd of elephants had run her over emotionally, she probably couldn't trust her impressions much. A half hour earlier she hadn't ever wanted to see Virgil or Aidan again. Now, however, with Aidan throwing out the cold reality of the three of them going their separate ways, she knew she wouldn't be able to stand that. The war had given her a taste of life without them, and she didn't care for it. Which was why she was willing to put aside her hurt feelings for now and see what could be done.

Virgil, who usually had something to say regardless of whether he should or not, seemed to be at a loss for where to begin.

"Thanks for putting me on the spot," he murmured, running his hands through the dark shag of his hair. "Thinking about something like this is one thing. Telling you about it, that's something else." He looked at them in turn. "And considering how long I've thought about this, you'd think I'd have the words."

This wasn't some spur-of-the-moment idea he was throwing out. "How long?" she asked hesitantly.

"Awhile," he said easily. "Are you telling me it's never crossed either of your minds? Not once?"

"Not as such," Aidan replied.

"Even with all that reading you've done?" Virgil pressed.

Aidan shook his head. "Dickens and Twain don't really get into that. Though if you looked at it right, maybe Shakespeare did. But with regards to you and Drea, it's always been an either-or deal."

Virgil's attention turned to her and she threw up her hands. "I didn't think...it wasn't...no."

"So when you've been with either one of us, you've never even thought about the one who wasn't there?" Virgil asked.

She thought back to their conversation the night before.

"That's not the same."

"Isn't it?" Virgil quirked an eyebrow. "As close as we've been over the years, it's hard to keep the third out when it's any two of us together. Be it guilt or comparison or feeling that something's missing."

"It's completely different when all three of us are physically together," Aidan stated.

"Yeah, no guilt because no one is left out."

"Virgil." Aidan's tone was warning.

"I wasn't being flip."

No one left out. Drea mulled it over. Someone always got left out in the end. Aidan was right earlier when he said that three eventually became a crowd. Now she wondered why she had thought the idea would work. It was too easy a solution.

She felt herself sway unsteadily on her feet. A strong hand was on either side of her suddenly, holding her up.

"Drea?"

"What's wrong?"

She swallowed, taking a deep breath to fight down the tears that threatened to rise again. Aidan and Virgil looked at her with such concern, gray eyes on her left and brown on her right. "I wish today never happened. We'll never be able to make this right."

Only when Aidan's hand cupped her cheek, thumb brushing along the fine bone, did she realize she was crying after all. "Shh," he soothed. "Not never. We'll find a way, Drea, I promise."

She looked up at Aidan, feeling Virgil's solid presence behind her. And for the first time all night, she felt like something had gone right. Between them, like this, it felt good, less crazy and more like how they should be. She linked the

172

fingers of her right hand with those of Virgil's left wrapped loosely around her waist. Her left hand moved up to cover Aidan's against her cheek.

She acted on impulse, rising up on her toes to capture Aidan's mouth lightly with hers. It opened in surprise and she pressed on, turning the contact from a mere meeting to more. She felt Virgil tense behind her and Aidan start to pull away, but she held them both in place as she continued to entice Aidan into the kiss. Finally, he responded, a bit hesitant at first, but growing less so as she continued. She drew back with a sigh.

"Drea, what—"

"Don't say anything yet," she pleaded, tugging Virgil around.

His eyes were dark when he looked down at her. But when she moved in to kiss him, he met her halfway and wasn't hesitant, taking control from the instant contact was made. He was the one to withdraw, leaving her breathless between them. She barely registered what Virgil had done to her before Aidan pulled her back to him, claiming her mouth in a searing kiss, completely devoid of his earlier surprise and very different from any she had ever shared with him before. It had a lot of Virgil's intensity but was all Aidan. If Virgil left her breathless, Aidan left her weak when he drew away.

Virgil spoke up this time. "What's going on, Drea?" His voice was low, rumbling with a quiet roughness.

"I don't know," she admitted. It had been impulse, plain and simple. "But it felt right."

Virgil's face grew almost hopeful.

Aidan's mood was unreadable when he spoke. "That felt right, but does this?" And he pulled Virgil to him, laying claim with a hungry, demanding kiss that Virgil readily responded to.

The anger and hurt from earlier when she caught them flared but quickly died out, replaced by curiosity and a sense of awe. When it wasn't something she mistakenly stumbled upon, seeing the two of them together wasn't so shocking. They looked good together. Really good. Good enough to make her want to see more. Much more.

Chapter Nineteen

A part of Aidan couldn't believe he was kissing Virgil in front of Drea. The other part was too busy enjoying what he was doing to care. Drea's initial kiss had taken him by complete surprise, but when she turned to Virgil, it touched something deep inside that Aidan hadn't been aware of. Not jealousy, but possession and the desire to let them know that this was one place he would not be standing back. So when Virgil had released Drea, Aidan showed her that he was capable of every bit as much passion as either of them. And then he set about reminding Virgil of that very fact.

When Aidan pulled back finally, Virgil stared at him. "Christ, Aidan," he breathed. "You haven't done it like that for a while."

"It's been awhile since I felt the need to," he admitted before turning to see Drea's reaction.

Her mouth was slightly open, blue eyes bright and wide. She blinked, noticing his attention. "I didn't think that..." she trailed off. She licked her lips before continuing. Aidan found himself fascinated by the moisture highlighting them as she spoke again. "It's not something I thought I'd like to see. But I do."

"Drea, honey." Virgil's voice was rough with emotion when he spoke, reaching over to cup Drea's cheek. "You'd better be certain it's something you like to see, because that was barely even getting started."

"How can I know for certain until I *do* see more?" Challenge danced in her eyes.

Aidan chuckled. It was good to see that Drea could still be herself regardless of the strange place they found themselves in.

"Well answered," Virgil said with admiration, his hand trailing down her cheek to her neck and coming to rest on the soft junction between neck and shoulder. His thumb stroked idly at the peek of collarbone above her shirt. The touch wasn't ineffective; a slight blush started to color her cheeks.

She swallowed. "Putting the moves on me isn't the more I wanted to see," was her amused reprimand. Her focus shifted to Aidan. "Don't hold back on my account."

"No intention of it." He mimicked Virgil's move on her opposite cheek, taking his time to feel the flutter of her pulse as he stroked down her neck until his hand came to rest across from Virgil's. He then reached for Virgil's shirt and pulled the other man close, leaning forward until he was nose to nose with Virgil. "Going through with this, we don't hold back on any account. Agreed?"

Virgil nodded, their noses bumping slightly. "No holding back."

The kiss wasn't as frantic as their initial one, all fire and little finesse. Now it built gradually, Aidan delving in and Virgil meeting and pushing back. Aidan felt Virgil's fingers curl around his neck, pulling him closer, deepening the kiss as their tongues danced around and along each other. It was so easy to get lost in Virgil, but there was someone else to consider.

Still occupying Virgil's mouth with his own, Aidan moved the hand that had been resting by Drea's neck out past her shoulder and down until he captured her hand. Grasping it firmly, he pulled back from Virgil as he tugged Drea between them, half twisting her so her back came to rest against his chest. He wrapped his arms around her and held her close.

Looking at Virgil, he murmured in her ear, "Still thinking about it, or have you decided?"

Before she could reply, Virgil moved in, kissing her every bit as intensely as he and Aidan had been kissing. Aidan felt her tense at first and then relax into the assault, leaning forward for more. Which was when Virgil pulled back, taking Drea with him and turning her to face Aidan. He didn't even think as he took her back into his arms and resumed the kiss where Virgil had left off. She melted against him. It encouraged him, and he devoured her with a hunger he had kept in check with her before. He hadn't been afraid of scaring her off, but had never felt the raw need to be anything but tender with her. She was softer than Virgil but no less fierce. He grasped her waist tighter, needing her closer than was possible right now, reveling in the welcoming press of her stomach against his hardening cock. Her groan in response to the move pleased a deep, primal part of himself.

They were both short of breath by the time they broke apart.

After a moment she spoke, her voice rich and throaty. "Very much decided." She reached behind her for Virgil, who stepped close, caging her between them.

"And that was only the beginning," Virgil chuckled warmly.

Only the beginning. Aidan liked that. He leaned forward and caught Virgil's mouth with a quick, light kiss.

Between Aidan and Virgil once again, Drea's sense of contentment returned. All the pieces had finally fallen into place. And then there was the effect of two very aroused male bodies pressed against her. Being in the middle, she also felt less the voyeur than when they paid attention to each other. She was a part of their intimacy like this, not an intruder.

Speaking of being included, her boys had returned their attentions to her. Virgil had swept her hair to the side and was nibbling along the column of her neck, sending pleasant little shivers radiating from wherever his teeth and lips and tongue touched. As for Aidan, he was looking down at her with a sense of wonder, as if he couldn't believe she was going along with this. Instead of speaking, however, he took her mouth with his own once more, taking his time to savor the experience.

He tasted faintly of Virgil. She hadn't given much thought to taste before, one compared to the other, but now she realized there was a definite difference between them. It was hard to say with absolute certainty what exactly they each tasted of except that they each possessed something unique. Aidan was warm and understated, something that wrapped around you, soothed you. Virgil was almost spicy without being such. He made your senses perk up and take notice, not all that unlike Raymond, strong and sharp with—Drea quickly derailed that train of thought, focusing on Aidan again and the mix of his subtlety with Virgil's more demanding flavor. It was irresistible.

While she was occupied sampling Aidan, she felt Virgil's sure and steady hands work along the buttons that held her shirt closed. She gasped against Aidan's lips as Virgil worked beneath the fabric of her blouse and his hand settled firmly around her breast. Leaning back, she relished the heat of his skin on her own through the thin layer of her chemise. His thumb circled down to graze across the nipple, sending a tiny charge of electricity through her with each pass.

"They're such a perfect fit," he whispered, slightly awed, palm and fingers cupping around the soft flesh. "Beautiful."

Drea didn't think she had ever heard anything more flattering.

Dazed, she reached for one of Aidan's hands and brought it up to her free breast still hidden behind shirt and chemise. His hand settled tentatively at first and then pressed more insistently as he took in the weight and shape of it.

"Absolutely," he agreed.

She reveled in the sensations of two independent hands mapping out the contours of her body. It was a wholly unique experience for her.

But as wonderful as it was to be their sole focus, she suddenly wanted more, wanted to know what she could do to them in this new situation. She wondered if she could divide her attention equally between them. A task that seemed impossible when she found standing on her own two feet a great challenge in and of itself.

Drea focused on grounding herself, pulling back from the bliss offered by the myriad of sensations washing over her. She didn't really want to. Hell, staying between them wasn't bad. But her curiosity won out. Steeling herself, she brought her hands up to rest over Aidan's and Virgil's, stilling them and easing them away. When she stepped out from between them, they looked at her with a mixture of confusion and concern.

"I'm curious," she said by way of explanation. "Bear with me. Please."

"She's up to something," Virgil observed.

"Which means we should probably be frightened," added Aidan, his brown eyes warmer than usual with the appreciative light in them.

"Always." Her lips curled in pleasure. "Now, both of you, hush."

Virgil smirked but didn't make any further comment. Aidan simply nodded.

Tilting her head to the side, Drea considered them and moved to stand before Aidan. She reached up and slipped the buttons from the holes of his flannel work shirt. Down she went, one after the other, revealing his plain white undershirt by degrees. At his waistband, she tugged the shirt from his pants and finished unbuttoning it before sliding her hands back up along his chest. Once she reached his shoulders, her hands slipped under the material and pushed it over and down his arms. Gnawing at her lower lip, she moved on to his undershirt. She gathered the bottom hem in her fingers and lifted, pleased that he automatically raised his arms to let her remove it unhindered. Finally, Aidan was completely bare-chested, and she stood there, trailing her gaze over the planes and contours, half-memorizing what she saw. She was tempted to reach out and map him by touch, but not yet. If she started touching Aidan, she'd likely never get to Virgil.

She took a couple steps to the side until she was now before Virgil, his steel eyes piercing.

"Bear with me," she repeated and set about undressing him as she had Aidan. Though with him, her task was accomplished much more quickly as he wore a knit sweater instead of a button-up.

Finished, she backed up far enough to be able to take both of them in side by side. Virgil was a bit taller than Aidan, with an overall lean strength. Aidan's body was softer, broader, less clearly defined, but there was still the impression of power carefully hidden. His muscle wasn't on display as much as Virgil's. You had to get close to know that Aidan was as much a force as Virgil was.

She took a step forward and reached out, her left hand

coming to rest on Virgil's chest and her right on Aidan's. Running her fingers lightly along, Drea mapped out the varying terrain and textures she passed over. Virgil was mostly smooth to the touch, only a faint trail of dark hair leading the gaze ever downward. Aidan wasn't hairy by any means, but her fingers wove through a downy soft field of sandy curls that you couldn't see so much as feel; it was another layer, albeit a thin one, between Aidan and the world. It had never occurred to Drea how unassuming Aidan was, not only in manners and personality, but appearance as well. You had to really look at him to see him. Whereas with Virgil everything was laid out at first glance. That wasn't to say Virgil didn't have his own hidden depths, but they were considerably easier to get at than Aidan's.

"Drea, honey," Virgil broke her reverie, "you're going to drive us both crazy if you keep doing that."

Her hands, as if with minds of their own, had taken to skimming back and forth along either boy's stomach at the soft fleshy parts right at the waistbands. The skin and muscles seemed to flutter at her touch. "Oh!" She snatched her hands away.

Or tried to, but Aidan had caught her right wrist. "Don't stop." It was half-plea, half-command. The request, which she would have expected from Virgil, was made all the more powerful coming from Aidan.

"I won't stop." She dipped her fingers behind the waistband of his trousers, her other hand returning to Virgil to do the very same.

Drea focused on getting her left hand to cooperate as well as her right and worked to unfasten the buttons at the top of each pair of pants. She soon had their pants open and worked a hand in either side, fingers nudging against cotton-covered hardness that reacted almost instantaneously to her touch.

Aidan's breath caught. "Easy, girl, easy." She was surprised to see his eyes closed, face slightly scrunched as if thinking hard. His features soon relaxed and his brown eyes were a bit glassy when they reopened and focused on her. "Just go slow."

She grinned at how little it took for her to affect him.

Virgil seemed to be doing fine, with enough presence of mind to flash her a knowing half-smirk.

"What?" she asked.

"You're enjoying this entirely too much, Drea."

She twisted her hand so it wrapped around Virgil's cock as much as the material would allow. The smirk disappeared. She added a little more pressure as she moved her hand up and down and was pleased to feel him arch up into her touch.

"No, I don't think I could ever enjoy this *too* much."

Drea repeated the same action on Aidan, then began to alternate different strokes, varying pressures. Right then left, Aidan then Virgil. Taking things one step further, she worked her way beneath both pairs of underwear, feeling a slight thrill with initial unhindered contact. She hadn't gotten used to it yet, how flesh could be so solid and malleable at the same time. Her fingers circled fully around each length as she reacquainted herself with Aidan and Virgil's cocks by touch alone, this time able to make a direct comparison. She was surprised to discover that Aidan was thicker and slightly longer than Virgil. Somewhere along the way she had made up her mind that Virgil was the bigger of the two. Maybe some of that was due to the intensity of their first time. Hell, at that point, anything would have seemed huge.

She couldn't help the giggle that escaped.

"What?" they asked almost at the same time, voices both thick with effort.

The giggle became full-out laughter that wouldn't let go. Removing her hands from their pants, Drea stepped away to pull herself together. Their slightly wounded, mostly confused faces mixed with their half-dressed state suddenly seemed the most hilarious thing ever.

"Oh God, I'm sorry," she gasped an apology before another bout of laughter overtook her. If it hadn't been a couple hours since she'd had that last bit of whiskey at Raymond's, she'd swear she was drunk. When the boys made a move toward her, whether to help or throttle her, she held up her hand to stop them. "Just...just give me...a moment." She backed up until her legs connected with her father's old armchair, and she sat down hard.

Several deep breaths and she had no idea how long after, Drea finally felt enough in control to look at her friends again. "I'm sorry," she repeated and was relieved to find that the giggle fit or whatever it was had finally passed.

Aidan knelt next to her, having decided that she was safe enough to approach. "What's going on in that head of yours, Drea?" There was no accusation, only genuine concern.

"Maybe I'm a bit overwhelmed by all of this."

"Well, you have good reason," he reassured her.

Virgil, while not insensitive, was always one for a different tack. "You going to tell us what set you off there?"

That struck her as more embarrassing than the laughing jag itself. She chewed at her lower lip as her cheeks flamed. Before she could duck her head away, Virgil knelt next to Aidan and lifted her chin.

"It can't be that bad, can it?"

No worse than anything else that day, she supposed. Taking a deep breath and releasing it, she finally replied in a rush, "I was kind of comparing and was surprised that Aidan

183

was bigger."

That earned a laugh from Aidan. "You do beat all, Drea." He sobered slightly. "And flattering as the thought is, I think—no, I *know* you're mistaken."

Drea caught the quick shake of Virgil's head. "Our girl's right." They both looked at him in surprise. "What? I can't be man enough to admit that?"

"But you're not smaller than me," Aidan protested.

"I'd suggest we measure for an unbiased opinion, but seeing as we just got Drea to stop laughing..."

Drea very nearly choked on the laugh that threatened to rise, setting off a small coughing fit. "How about we go with the majority for now?"

"I would be stupid to press the issue, seeing as it is in my favor." Aidan's lips curled into a soft smile.

"Smart man." Virgil favored his friend with a grin. When he turned his focus back to Drea, she had no desire to laugh anymore. His face still held the good humor of the boy she had known forever, but his eyes were dark with the hunger and passion of a man she was barely starting to know. He leaned forward and tugged up the hem of her skirt. "You know exactly what I'm going to do, don't you, Drea?"

Yes she did. Her body responded automatically to the memories of the previous night, thighs clenching as she felt the wetness gather between her legs. It had been unlike anything she had experienced and never had she felt more vulnerable. She wasn't opposed to the idea of him doing it again, but to do it with Aidan watching? Her heart thudded at the thought. Part of her had no problem with it, but the more rational part of her had doubts. It wasn't something a person watched, was it? Well, unless you were a certain sort. And they weren't that sort of people, were they? But if they were going to be together, the three of them, at the same time, someone would be watching the others at some point, right? Oh. God.

"Drea." Aidan's warm tones cut through her chaotic thoughts, his hand solid and firm over hers, which was gripping the chair arm as if her life depended on it. She blinked, trying to focus on him. "If any of this is too much, just say the word."

"It's all right if it is." Virgil's hand caressed soothingly along her calf.

"It isn't too much for you?" she asked Aidan, needing his reassurance.

He ran his thumb lightly along the outside of her hand. "No, it's not. I'm well out of my depth, but it's far from too much."

She looked at Virgil. "Do you know how all of this is going to work out?"

"I have a vague idea, but for the most part I'm making it up as I go." Virgil's admission was extremely comforting in that, while he knew more than her or Aidan, he wasn't completely confident, either. That decided her.

"Keep going."

Virgil nodded and continued from where he left off.

Drea forced herself to relax against the back of the chair. She twisted the hand beneath Aidan's reassuring grip so she could grasp his in return.

"We'll figure this out together," he said quietly, squeezing her hand.

Their situation had changed, but the friendship remained. It was good to know.

Virgil had always been proud of his ability to remain confident regardless of how insecure or uncertain he was. If things were going to get anywhere between the three of them, someone had to act like they knew what they were doing. And he was the most likely candidate, thanks to the "education" his uncle had insisted upon at Madam Violet's. While he would never tell the man to his face, Virgil was grateful for those trips down to Grand Rapids. Even more so once he and Aidan had started fooling around.

Virgil had confided in Madam Violet during his visit there the winter following the Bill Wellington incident. One too many drinks and thinking about it too much had led to a slip of his tongue. Before his mouth could run away with him, she had ushered him upstairs to her private rooms and sat patiently while he confessed to her. She reassured him that he had nothing to be ashamed of and proceeded to show him over the course of the weekend, and to the best of her abilities, what exactly was available to him with Aidan if he continued to pursue it.

He really had to thank her for that one of these days, especially if he managed to get this to work with the three of them. But right now he had better things to be thinking about. Better things to be doing. Such as freeing Drea by degrees from the confines of her clothing.

Skimming his hands down her calves, he slipped his fingers under the barrier of her woolen socks and pushed them to bunch around her ankles. He focused his attention on her right foot first, lifting it and tugging the sock off by the toes, slowly uncovering the pale skin beneath. Next came the left, which he continued to hold long after he tossed the sock aside, studying the callus under her middle toe and the way her arch curved just so. He was pulled back to the present by an impatient wiggling of Drea's toes.

"Is my foot really that fascinating?" she asked, amusement evident.

186

"You didn't know Virgil had a foot fetish?" Aidan sounded so serious that Virgil had to look at him to know that he was joking.

"Watch it, Morrison," he warned as he abandoned Drea's foot to the floor. He let his hands trail up her legs to where her skirt lay rolled and resting on her knees. "Or I can let you figure out how to do this yourself."

Aidan was unfazed. "Something tells me I could manage."

"He has really good instincts." Drea's voice was low and enticing.

Virgil's cock responded to both comment and voice. Aidan did indeed have good instincts, instincts that had taken over when Madam Violet's teachings hadn't been enough. And Drea, God, it was fortunate she didn't sound like that all the time when she talked, or he'd never leave her alone.

"How come I get ganged up on here?" he protested as he inched Drea's skirt higher until the bottoms of her drawers were visible.

"Because you're taking your sweet time," she replied.

"And it's fun," Aidan chimed in.

"Just once," Virgil said as he brought the hem of Drea's skirt to rest at her waist and reached up to tug the tie on her drawers free, "it would be nice for one of you to side with me." He tugged the cotton down, revealing the soft, white expanse of her stomach. He worked the material as low as was physically possible before continuing. "Or maybe help me out from time to time? A man can't do *everything* by himself."

"Aidan may have instincts, but you're pretty creative. I'm sure you could think of some way to help yourself if you had to." Drea's eyes danced.

"I could, but I really don't want to right now." The last part he said with only a faint hint of levity.

Bracing herself on the arms of the chair, Drea lifted her rear from the seat enough so he could slip her drawers the rest of the way off. For all the teasing, it was obvious she was still uncertain from the slight tremor in her stomach and the way her legs pressed closer together to retain a little modesty once she sat back down. Confronted with her laid bare before him, Virgil realized how terrified *he* was to be doing this. He had been anxious before, but it hadn't been so very real until now. Christ, he was going to eat Drea out in front of Aidan and, while they were also nervous, they didn't seem to be afraid of forging ahead.

He brought his hands to rest on Drea's knees. All joking was laid aside when he spoke. "Are you absolutely certain you're okay with me doing this now?"

She was silent before she replied quietly, "Yes, Virgil, I am."

He looked to Aidan, but the other man beat him to the punch. "Yes, Virgil, I'm all right with this."

"Fuck," he exhaled. They were good and he was, well mostly good. So what was he waiting for?

Slowly, he prized Drea's legs open, amazed that she didn't resist him at all. The white flesh of her thighs parted, gradually revealing the entirety of her coppery curls and the sensitive pink flesh normally carefully hidden but now displayed, glistening slightly with her arousal. He was a very fortunate man.

He ran his palms up along the soft skin of her inner thighs, feeling every goose bump that his touch elicited. Up he went until there was no farther to go. Fingers splayed, middle fingers nudging her hipbones, his thumbs hovered over her pussy, waiting the barest of moments before making contact. First his left then right thumb traced down her slit, skating over the slick, satiny flesh begging to be touched. He pushed apart her labia, baring the delicacies of her sex completely unhindered to his hungry gaze. Without further thought, Virgil bowed worshipfully, bringing his mouth achingly close to his target. He blew lightly over the flesh just to hear Drea's sharp intake of breath at the teasing contact before his tongue darted out and he ran it flat and firm over the swollen flesh to take the first taste of her. It was a heady flavor, mostly salty and a little sweet with something indescribable that made him crave more. So more he took. He explored every fold and ridge, savoring what he had been unable to in his determination last night to show Drea what she had no idea of. He held her hips firmly grounded to the chair as she tried to rise up. Her body was his. All his for just this moment. Every gasp and moan, the flood of juices that coated his tongue as he licked and probed.

"God...Virgil...I don't think...I...oh, fuck..." Her choked exclamations barely filtered over the rush of blood in his ears, of the desire driving him. He could push her over so easily. But he'd already had that surrender from her once and, while he desperately wanted to drive her to it again, that wasn't his goal.

He tore himself away, sat back on his heels and took in her shock at being abandoned so abruptly.

Aidan spoke up. "Virgil, what are you—"

Virgil wrapped a hand behind Aidan's neck and pulled him forward, cutting off the words as Aidan's lips touched his own. Aidan made as if to draw back, but Virgil held him there, forcing Aidan to open to him. The low groan Aidan gave as he accepted the assault was almost more satisfying than Drea's gasping pleas. But even that wasn't as good as when Aidan took control of the kiss, pulling Virgil close as his tongue darted in and out and around Virgil's mouth, tasting the rewards of Virgil's labors.

"Delicious, isn't she?" Virgil asked, his voice gone rough.

"Jesus." It was said with absolute wonder. "It's kind of like how you taste, but..."

"Better?" Virgil grinned.

"Different. Good different. But not better or worse," Aidan replied softly. His head turned toward Drea. "I don't think you can compare it."

Drea looked slightly bemused. "I'll take your word on that."

Aidan then asked her, "Would you mind if I tried?"

Her cheeks grew pinker, but her voice was steady when she replied. "If you want to."

"Virgil?"

"That's why I stopped, Aidan. Drea's willing and waiting." He pointedly moved to the side, leaving the way open.

Aidan blushed as he moved to kneel between Drea's legs. He glanced sheepishly at Virgil. "How do I do this?"

"Go slow and easy. The terrain's a bit different, but the idea's the same."

"Right." Aidan's brow furrowed as he swallowed hard. Then he faced Drea. "You all right?"

"I will be when one of you decides to do something for me." The words were pointed but gentle.

As Aidan leaned down to taste Drea directly for the first time, Virgil realized that compared to Aidan, he hadn't been nervous at all. Aidan's uncertainty was clear in the stiff set of his shoulders, the tension visible in the tight muscles of his neck.

"Just remember our first time together," Drea murmured to Aidan, running her right hand lightly through his hair. "It took some trial and error, but we soon figured out what to do, right?"

Virgil saw Aidan's shoulders relax slightly as he finally committed to action. He must have found a sensitive place because Drea gasped sharply. He started to pull back, but she held him in place, murmuring for him to keep on. It was no small amount of jealousy that Virgil felt watching Drea and Aidan together. They had shared something that Virgil wasn't a part of, couldn't be a part of. And then again, he couldn't begrudge them the connection, either. They each had their connections with one or the other that the third could never quite share. It was why they had become friends to begin with. No one of them had everything the others needed. Like here, Drea and Aidan had their inexperience in common, but Virgil had enough insight to guide them when needed. The flare of jealousy quickly ceded to fascination. It was beautiful watching them together.

He couldn't help smiling when Drea came, eyes fluttering closed as she gasped out a hoarse, "Oh, God, Aidan."

Virgil felt the same amount of satisfaction in Aidan's accomplishment as if he'd done it himself.

Chapter Twenty

Once his nervousness abated, Aidan found that Virgil's claim of different-terrain-but-same-idea held true. Drea's quiet, breathless encouragements helped guide him when all else failed. He pulled away with great reluctance when Drea finally stilled. It was so new and fascinating, he found himself loath to end the experience. And, God, but she tasted so good. Sex and salt and heat. Very much like Virgil tasted when he came, and not like Virgil at all. Aidan wiped at his mouth automatically, transferring the lingering juices from face to hand. So wet. Feeling it when he fucked her was one thing, but tasting it and being there...he didn't have the words.

"I remember you talking about it plenty, but it never occurred to me to try it myself." He broke the silence that had descended.

"But you're glad you did." There was a hint of question in Virgil's statement.

"Yeah, I really am," he said reassuringly, transfixed by the way the moisture on his hand caught the light.

A rustling came from the chair as Drea sat up, her skirt tumbling down between her legs to hide her from view once more. "You sure you haven't done that before?"

"Good instincts, I guess."

She laughed. "I'd lean more toward great, but good works, too."

Only when he moved to relieve the tingling in his feet from sitting on them did Aidan became aware of the fact that the effects of the encounter weren't only cerebral. He'd forgotten about himself entirely, but now that his attention wasn't fully focused on Drea, he realized how incredibly hard he was.

"Could I maybe..." Drea stopped, rethinking her words. "I think I'd like to... Oh, hell," she sighed.

"What's going on, Drea?" Aidan jumped in, thankful for the distraction that pulled his focus elsewhere.

"It's going to sound crazy after the way I reacted this afternoon," she said sheepishly.

Virgil chuckled. "Honey, we've gone a bit past crazy here, so there's no harm in speaking what's on your mind."

The color rising on her cheeks showed her discomfort more than her nervous shifting did. At last, she mustered her courage. "Well, I'd kind of like to see the two of you with each other again."

"What you saw in the workshop or..." Virgil prompted.

"Maybe. Or something else. Whatever you two want, I guess." She fiddled with the fabric of her skirt.

Virgil smirked. "That's leaving things pretty wide open. You sure you don't maybe want to qualify that a bit?"

Drea gave a quick shake of her head. "No, I leave it completely up to you."

Virgil a solid force behind him, chest hard and ungiving against his back and fucking him at a quick pace, driving thought and breath from him in equal measure—Aidan shoved the image away, embarrassed to realize how hard he was breathing.

"Aidan, are you all right?" Drea leaned forward.

"Yeah, fine." His voice cracked slightly.

"What is it, Aidan?" Virgil pressed, but it wasn't out of concern. No, Aidan would wager that Virgil had a pretty good idea what had been going through his head. Christ, had it only been yesterday when he'd visited Virgil in the carriage house? Though yesterday, Aidan had fucked Virgil. He hadn't been fucked by Virgil since right after they'd enlisted, nearly two years gone now. The only time things had been safe enough during the war, he'd had his breakdown above the goddamned bar in Deuxoreilles.

The more he thought about Virgil fucking him, the more he wanted it. But that wouldn't be the best thing to do in front of Drea. The way he and Virgil got with each other when they were alone wasn't something she needed to see yet. But he was less worried about shocking Drea so much as being *that* vulnerable in front of her, letting her see how much he enjoyed it.

"No," he whispered. "Not like that, not tonight."

"If not tonight, then when, Aidan? Drea left the door wide open for us." He knew it wouldn't be enough to put Virgil off. Virgil was worse that a pit bull that way; once he sunk his teeth into something, there was nothing for it but to let him have his way.

Drea slipped from the chair and knelt before him. She placed her hand gently on his cheek. "I meant what I said. Anything. I'm no blushing virgin, Aidan. And I wasn't much for the blushing when I was one." She gave him a soft smile. "Remember how annoying I got, begging both you and Virgil to let him tell me all that went on at Madam Violet's?"

He couldn't help smiling in acknowledgment. If Virgil was a pit bull, Drea was even worse. Hell, if Virgil and Drea hadn't been at odds with each other most of the time, Aidan never would have stood a chance against them.

In all seriousness, he finally told her, "I want him to fuck me, Drea. I want it so bad, I can practically taste it." He didn't miss how her eyes grew wider. "Sometimes it's gentle. But often it's not. It's desperate and rough. And it's a side of me I don't know as I want you to see."

She stayed silent for the longest of moments. Aidan was almost certain he'd dissuaded her. Her steady, simple reply cured him of that notion. "I really wish you'd let me see it."

His heart stopped. She wasn't bluffing.

"He's not exaggerating, Drea. Two men together ain't always pretty," Virgil said soberly. "So you better be damn sure."

Two words, undeniable: "I am." Then she reminded them, "Didn't we set out into this with the idea there would be no holding back? Well, don't hold back."

If he'd ever doubted it before, Aidan knew he'd never doubt again that he loved Drea Samuels beyond all reason.

Virgil stood and held out a hand to each of them. "Come on." He tugged first Drea and then Aidan to their feet.

Aidan followed them in a sort of daze. He found it very difficult to believe that any of this was really happening. That's not to say he thought it was a dream. Everything was too real. Maybe it was the too realness of it that made it so difficult to accept. He'd gone down on Drea with Virgil watching and now Virgil was going to fuck him with Drea watching.

"Drea, go make yourself comfortable on the bed," he heard Virgil direct her.

"Comfortable how?" she queried.

"Just comfortable."

Aidan saw her give Virgil a half-threatening look.

He held up his hands in defense. "I'm not being cagey.

Whatever you think is comfortable."

She frowned, a tiny crease appearing between her eyebrows. "All right." She slipped the mostly undone shirt the rest of the way off and her skirt after. Left only with her thin underdress, she grabbed up the spare blanket from the bottom of the bed, wrapped it around herself and proceeded to the top of the bed and snuggled up against the headboard. She regarded them, eyes wide and clear. "Well, I'm comfortable," she said with a hint of impatience.

Virgil murmured, "With a vengeance, too." Then he reached for Aidan, shifting his focus.

Aidan let the other man tug him close. They stood toe-to-toe and all he could think to say as he stared into Virgil's stormy gaze was, "Damn."

Virgil's hand rose to cup his cheek briefly before caressing down his neck and coming to rest on his shoulder. "This is going to be awkward as hell at first. But once we relax into it, I don't think it'll be so bad."

"Your move," Aidan said, more plea than statement. He needed Virgil's confidence now.

Virgil nodded and moved the hand up from Aidan's shoulder to curl around his neck and pulled Aidan to him. The kiss was gentler than Aidan expected from Virgil in these kinds of situations. When they fooled around, there was more instinct than thought going on. That was the key, stop thinking. So Aidan shoved his worries and analyses to the side and kissed Virgil back, harder, hungrier. And Virgil didn't mind at all, his grip tightening, fingers digging into Aidan's neck as he matched Aidan's intensity.

Aidan ghosted his hands around Virgil's sides, roaming over his back and down to settle on his ass. Holding Virgil in place, Aidan ground his hips forward, groaning in relief and need when his cock rubbed against Virgil's through the layers of clothing still between them. Their shirts had been long ago removed by Drea, but their pants, while undone, were still frustratingly in place.

"Need to feel more," he breathed against Virgil's ear, moving his hands up to push at the waistband of Virgil's pants.

Virgil's free hand found its way to the top of Aidan's pants, slipping past that layer and the next to rest promisingly on bare skin, fingers teasing downward. "I couldn't agree more," was the hoarse response.

They worked together, each divesting the other of their remaining clothing. Naked finally, Aidan pulled Virgil to him, shuddering as their bare cocks brushed against each other. He showed his pleasure by losing himself in Virgil's mouth, kissing him like there was no tomorrow. And maybe there wouldn't be.

Virgil broke the connection, fingers tangling in Aidan's hair and angling his head back, baring his throat. Working down the column, Virgil murmured, between licks and teasing bites, "How do you want to do this?"

"Hm?" Aidan tried to pull together some semblance of coherent thought.

"When I fuck you"—the words sounded reverent to Aidan's ears—"do you want to see me or Drea?"

Virgil's question flooded Aidan with an odd mix of awareness and arousal. He'd forgotten they weren't alone. Now that he was reminded, he became very alert to the fact. Craning his neck against Virgil's grip, Aidan saw Drea still curled up at the head of the bed. But she wasn't sitting demurely, watching. He'd never seen her eyes so big and dark, the blue having moved from the shallows to the deeps, and her chest rose and fell with short, quick movements. God, he was fascinated by the effect he and Virgil had on her.

"I..." He swallowed hard. "I want to see what we do to her."

Virgil's response was a low, rich laugh as he maneuvered Aidan to look at him once more. "Me, too." And then he kissed Aidan hard and demanding, driving all breath and rationality from Aidan. Virgil spun Aidan so back was to chest. Aidan was very aware of the hardness resting promisingly against his ass. Virgil's chin came to rest on his shoulder. "Don't you think it's time we showed her what this was about?"

Aidan could only nod.

Virgil nudged him toward the bed. "Get on the bed, hands and knees, I'll be right back." Virgil stepped away, leaving Aidan's back cold.

Finally, Aidan spurred himself into motion, slowly joining Drea on the bed but careful to keep a distance between them. Without Virgil nearby, Aidan found himself a little more capable of speech. "Still fine with this?"

"Yeah. But my brain stopped working a while ago, so I'm not sure how much you can believe that."

"Thinking is overrated, Drea," he said, happy to see her lips curl in delight.

"So yours isn't working much either," she teased.

"Which is a very good thing."

"Your brains seem to be working enough for the two of you to jabber on with me out of the room," Virgil observed from the doorway.

Aidan glanced back to see Virgil holding a bottle of Drea's bath oil in his right hand. Sure as hell beat the carriage house yesterday. Spit worked in a pinch but was far from perfect. They'd learned that lesson the hard way.

With a grin, Aidan moved into position and waited.

The oil was warmer than he'd expected, though he still

shivered from the contact as it trailed between his cheeks. Anticipation was almost his favorite part of the act, the knowing what to expect, craving it, but not knowing exactly how this time would be different from the others. Because every time was different. Sometimes frenzied, sometimes slow. Driven by lust or maybe a touch of anger, the sheer enjoyment of it or any other number of emotions. He was breathing raggedly by the time one of Virgil's fingers slid teasingly along the cleft of his ass. A small moan escaped unbidden as Virgil began to circle the pucker concealed there.

"Just getting started," Virgil stated, voice heavy with the promise of more.

Aidan fisted his hands in the blankets and forced himself not to glance at Drea. He couldn't handle her reaction, whatever it was. He needed to ignore her for the time being, otherwise he was going to be a nervous wreck.

"Don't drag it out," he told Virgil.

"I won't." Virgil's free hand rested comfortingly on Aidan's lower back. The finger teasing Aidan's hole worked its way inward. "But I'm not rushing, either."

Virgil found that happy medium that was quick enough to keep Aidan focused on the sensations but slow enough to savor as well. The gradual breach reacquainted both of them with the way this was done. It was barely enough to stretch, to get used to things. When Virgil moved in and out with increasingly deeper thrusts, Aidan felt himself relax as the first tiny frissons of pleasure washed over him.

"More," he said, his voice still fairly even.

Virgil complied, and Aidan felt the subtle sting of being stretched almost too much as Virgil added a second finger. Almost too much but far from enough. The penetration changed slightly, the smooth in and out mixed with subtle scissoring apart of fingers, intensifying the sensations.

"God, Virgil," he cried out as Virgil's fingers twisted just so, glancing off his prostate. Virgil did it again and Aidan gasped, "Need you. Now. Please."

"Not much longer," Virgil soothed, the hand on Aidan's back moving in a comforting caress.

"Now," Aidan demanded, fighting the urge to look at Drea. She hadn't made a sound. Was she completely horrified? Virgil fucking him had been a mistake, hadn't it? His thoughts came to an abrupt halt as Virgil's fingers slipped from his ass without warning. But before Aidan could voice his protest at the loss, he felt the smooth head of Virgil's cock nudging against his entrance. And then Virgil was pressing inside, steadily filling Aidan. "Yes," Aidan groaned, the faint burning completely overridden by the sheer pleasure of having Virgil inside him after all this time.

"So hot and tight," Virgil murmured brokenly behind him.

When Virgil was firmly seated, Aidan barely had a chance to enjoy the feeling before Virgil's arm wrapped around his waist, easing him up onto his knees until his back was flush with Virgil's chest. The change in angle stretched Aidan more, making him feel fuller. He groaned, letting his head fall back against Virgil's shoulder, eyes fluttering closed. "Yeah, that's good."

Virgil's chest vibrated with quiet laughter. "You are far too easy to please, Aidan."

"Fine one to talk, you are."

"You keep telling yourself that." Aidan then felt Virgil's mouth against his ear, tongue teasing at the lobe. "Open your eyes, Aidan, and look at our girl."

If Virgil was telling him to look, it couldn't be that bad. But looking at Drea would bring reality crashing back. He was being fucked by Virgil in front of Drea. God, that was…he swallowed down his fear and forced his eyes open, zeroing in on her. What little breath he still had immediately fled at the sight of her. The blanket had fallen from her shoulders, revealing a warm, rosy flush to the skin not hidden by her thin chemise. He made out the dark circles of her nipples pebbled hard and moving against the fabric of her shift in time with her breath. His gaze traveled upward, lingering at where her pulse beat madly at the vulnerable skin of her neck. Up farther to her lips, red and slightly parted, teeth barely visible. Lastly he found her eyes, even darker than before, pupils wide and straining against the blue surrounding them. She blinked and then noticed his observations.

That was when Virgil withdrew almost completely before slamming his cock back inside in one, quick stroke. The only sound Aidan was capable of was the quiet whoosh of his breath leaving him at the intensity of what Virgil had done. Somehow Drea seemed every bit as affected.

Aidan licked his lips and never took his eyes from Drea when he told Virgil with as much force as he could muster, "Again."

Virgil's teeth nipped at Aidan's ear, tugging lightly. "As if I could ever deny you," he whispered roughly and proceeded to fuck Aidan with sure, steady strokes, building in speed and intensity as he repeated his actions again and again and again.

Aidan lifted his right arm, curling it back around Virgil, fingers weaving through soft, dark hair, seeking purchase to hold him close. Aidan's left hand reached blindly for Virgil's, found it at his hip and guided it to his aching, unattended cock.

"Bring me off with you," he begged, hissing with pleasure as Virgil's still slightly slick hand curled with sure familiarity around his shaft.

Emery Sanborne

Aidan lost himself in Drea's eyes, in the feel of Virgil in him and around him. He lost all sense of time and reality as the sensations built higher and higher, leaving him capable of only feeling and the most primal of grunts and groans.

Virgil tensed behind him and gave a few more jerky thrusts before coming hard and hot inside him. It was enough to tip Aidan over the edge as his own release spilled wetly against his stomach.

They clung to each other after, until their bodies regained some semblance of normal. Drea moved before either of them, slipping off the bed and disappearing from view. Aidan didn't get a chance to wonder where she went as Virgil chose that moment to withdraw from him, leaving Aidan pleasantly aching and very empty. He turned enough to see Virgil, who looked as dazed as Aidan felt.

"Damn," Aidan said finally.

Virgil nodded. "About sums it up."

"I, um…" The hesitant voice at the other end of the room caught their attention. Drea was standing outside the bathroom, a couple towels clutched to her chest. Her color was still very high. She shifted her weight from one foot to the other and back again. "I…Is it—oh, I don't know. Is it always that intense?"

Aidan looked at Virgil who nodded, so Aidan went ahead and replied, "Yeah, pretty close."

She blinked and swallowed hard before finally crossing the room to them. Holding out a towel to each of them, she said softly, "I'm glad."

Aidan felt his brows draw together in confusion and saw a similar look on Virgil's face.

"I kind of, um"—she glanced at the floor and then back at them in turn—"really liked it."

202

"You did?" Virgil asked.

"Yes," she said definitively.

"You're amazing, Drea," was all Aidan could think to say, but it summed things up quite well. If she was able to accept, even like, him and Virgil together, maybe this new dynamic between the three of them could work after all.

She leaned forward and kissed him lightly, tongue teasing before she pulled away and switched her attentions to Virgil. Then she stepped back and regarded them, hands on hips and every line of her radiated the feisty girl she had been and the formidable woman she had become. "You're damn lucky to have me," she stated, amusement coloring her tone. "And if you care about keeping me, you'll both get cleaned up and come back here so we can finish talking. All right?"

Sometimes, it was smart to let Drea have her way.

Chapter Twenty-one

Drea scrunched her eyes against the pale, early sun. Mornings always came too soon for her taste, especially in the winter. She was not looking forward to getting up from her warm, cozy bed to dress for the day. The sun didn't seem all that high yet. She could probably get away with putting the day off for a little while longer.

Turning over, she was very intent on snuggling down and drifting off until her outstretched arm brushed against something that was definitely not her pillow. Drea's eyes shot open, and she gave a start when she saw Aidan's brown eyes staring sleepily back. Concern immediately replaced sleepiness as his hand came up to rest comfortingly on her shoulder.

"Drea?" His voice was soft and quiet.

The shock of finding herself not alone in bed did wonders to wake her up, and as awareness returned so did her memory of the events of the previous night.

She smiled sheepishly. "I fell asleep, didn't I?"

"Dead to the world by the time we got back." He grinned and stroked his thumb idly along her skin.

While Aidan and Virgil had been busy cleaning up in the washroom, Drea had bided her time waiting for them. She remembered thinking she'd catch a quick nap and that they'd rouse her when they were done.

"Did you even try to wake me up?" She was disappointed. Things had been going really well, then she'd gone and fallen asleep.

"We did, but after you nearly gave Virgil a black eye, we decided it was probably better to let you sleep."

She had never cared for being woken up against her will. Her daddy had given her hell about it a number of times over the years, said it wasn't ladylike. One time she told him it was his own damned fault for making her as stubborn as he was. It was one of the few occasions he'd taken a hand to her. After the incident, she'd gotten even worse about getting up in the mornings.

"Sorry," she said.

Aidan shrugged. "It was pretty late. Probably for the best."

"I wouldn't go that far," mumbled a voice from behind her. She craned her neck to see Virgil lying on his back, eyes closed.

She sat up and peered down at him. "Well, you only have yourselves to blame for letting me intimidate you like that. If you'd really wanted to wake me up, you wouldn't have given up so easy."

He snorted. "Honey, you don't get up until you're good and ready. Doesn't matter what anyone tries. Mind you, I had some good ideas, but they'd be a hell of a lot more enjoyable with you wide awake and not mad as hell."

"The man makes a good point," Aidan agreed.

Virgil chuckled. "At least now I've finally figured out the secret to getting you to take my side, Aidan."

The image of them locked together, lost in each other but still somehow managing to have eyes only for her, flared up in Drea's mind. She had to remind herself how to breathe. Here they were, the three of them, lying in her bed and talking like things were the same as ever. Even after everything. Oddly enough, it didn't feel all that different from the sleepovers they'd had in the Morrison hayloft growing up, except the boys were completely naked now. Both of them naked, in her bed, with her, and it didn't feel strange.

"You know," she mused, "pretty much about this time yesterday I was thinking we were done for. By the afternoon, I was convinced of it."

"And now?" Aidan sat up, turning toward her.

"Now it doesn't feel like anything was ever wrong."

The bed shifted as Virgil propped himself up. "Funny how things work out, isn't it?"

"Speaking of things working out," Aidan prompted, though he sounded reluctant about doing such.

Aidan, ever the voice of reason. Drea doubted they'd make it very far without him.

"You would go and ruin the morning," Virgil groused.

Drea smacked him on the chest.

"Hey!"

She flashed him a stern look. "Don't be an ass right now, Virgil."

"Yes, Mother," he muttered. There was a wicked glint in his eye. She was about to protest when he pulled her down and claimed her mouth. The thought of resisting him crossed her mind briefly until he did something with his tongue that made her want to fall into him. He released her finally, letting her sit up, breathless and very aroused.

Aidan was entirely too amused. So, she acted on the first idea that came to mind. She leaned forward and kissed him with the same intensity Virgil had shown her. Aidan conceded immediately. His hands settled about her waist and pulled her toward him. Half-crawling, she wound up straddling him and pressed close as his arms wrapped tight about her. The way her shift had ridden up, there was nothing between them, and she felt his cock slip along her slit.

"Need you," he groaned, sounding so desperate.

Drea's eyes darted to Virgil. "Do you really think I have any right to complain?"

No, she supposed, he really didn't.

She turned her attention back to Aidan. Reaching between them, she lightly wrapped her fingers around his cock and guided it toward her center. Capturing his mouth again, she thrust her hips downward, sheathing him fully in one clean stroke.

"God, I don't think I realized how much *I* needed that," she gasped, reveling in the feel of him stretching and filling her.

Aidan looked to be in complete ecstasy. His right hand came up and combed lightly through her hair. "Girl, you have no idea how amazing you feel."

The comment left her with a warm, content feeling in the pit of her stomach.

So focused was she on Aidan that she didn't notice Virgil moving until his hands settled on her upper thighs. The heat from the contact only intensified as his fingers hooked under the hem of her shift and began to draw it up and off of her.

"This is really only going to get in the way," he whispered conspiratorially.

"What are you doing?" she asked as Aidan's arms moved away from her long enough to let Virgil remove the garment.

"Don't you worry about that," Virgil replied, placing a faint kiss at the base of her neck. "You just worry about Aidan right now."

He was up to something. But she wasn't given the chance to be curious for long as Aidan pulled her close for a quick, teasing kiss, the movement bringing her now bare breasts into contact with the soft hairs of his chest.

Pulling back, he licked his lips and held her gaze steady. When he spoke, his words seemed very deliberate. "I want you to start moving nice and slow. Small, easy movements."

His behavior was even more curious than Virgil's.

"Because there's no reason to rush."

Drea was suspicious but shrugged the feeling off and did as Aidan requested. She rose up, the slight withdrawal of his cock causing an almost too intense sensation after being still for so long.

"Like that," Aidan said soothingly, hands settling on her hips to help guide her.

Taking things at such a pace made her more aware of every sensation, not only the feel of Aidan inside of her, but the way her muscles flexed and released, the weight of his hands on her, the feel of his skin under her hands, the—

"What in the hell are you doing?" she shrieked, body immediately tensing as she felt a slick finger probing between her ass cheeks. Aidan's hands were still firmly locked on her hips. "Virgil, what are you doing?"

"Trust me," he crooned, chest resting lightly against her back. One of his arms wrapped loosely around her, hand stroking soothing circles over her stomach. The other hand remained where it was, finger where it had initially captured her attention. "This is going to be good, I promise."

She finally realized exactly what he was doing. Oh. That was, um... She really didn't know.

"You can do that to me while Aidan's in me?" Her voice was

strained. She had trouble thinking beyond the finger slowly circling, pressing in and then retreating before circling again. Her body started to relax even while her mind couldn't quite make sense of what was going on.

"Yes." His breath tickled across her skin.

"It'll feel good?"

"Yes, it will," both Virgil and Aidan replied together.

Then Aidan added, "It's strange at first but gets better as you get used to it."

"Focus on Aidan," Virgil instructed. "The less you think about what I'm doing back here, the sooner you'll enjoy this."

Aidan's left hand came up under her chin, lifting it and drawing her focus. "Keep your eyes on mine. Don't look away."

She nodded once.

"Good. Now start moving again."

Drea resumed the agonizingly slow pace she'd been at before Virgil interrupted. The more she moved, the less attention she paid to what Virgil was doing. Until he slipped a finger inside. She froze again.

"Drea, keep moving." Aidan's voice held a commanding note that she felt compelled to obey.

Then Virgil's finger moved, withdrawing as she descended on Aidan and returned as she rose up. And she realized it wasn't half bad. The more he did it, the more she liked it. Different but good. Until he added another finger, and then all she felt was pain and burning. But he didn't let up.

"Drea." Aidan's sharp voice demanded her attention. "It will pass. Trust us."

She blinked at the tears stinging her eyes, forcing them back, forcing down the panic, forcing herself to concentrate on Aidan and moving.

Virgil spoke, his voice a steady anchor. "Breathe as you move, it helps. Advice direct from Madam Violet."

In spite of everything, Drea smiled at his words. "Well"—she swallowed—"who am I to argue with Madam Violet?"

The strange good feeling returned and Virgil began moving his fingers in counterpoint to her movements on Aidan again.

"It does get better," she conceded.

"Not done yet." Virgil's words were both a promise and a warning.

The third finger hurt, but not as much as the second one had. Maybe because she knew what to expect.

She cried out when he removed the fingers altogether, not from pain but from the loss.

"Relax," Virgil said. She felt the bed shift as he moved behind her, then she felt the unmistakable press of the head of his cock against the hole his fingers had abandoned.

"Drea, relax." Aidan pulled her attention again. "And remember, he's smaller than me."

Her grin was lost as Aidan kissed her, hungry and demanding, leaving her unable to think beyond him and his mouth on hers as he pulled her down on the bed with him. He swallowed down her cry as Virgil finally pressed in. Virgil might be smaller than Aidan, but he wasn't tiny by any stretch of her imagination, or stretch of anything else for that matter. And then he was in completely, tight against her back. As she grew used to the new sensation, she realized that it felt very, very right. Being between them felt right.

Aidan released her mouth so she could catch her breath.

Virgil whispered in her ear. "Now it gets really good." At which point he pulled out and thrust in, which in turn forced her up Aidan's cock and down again as Virgil withdrew once more.

It was a similar rhythm to what they had established earlier. She was never without one of them fully inside her at any point in time.

"Amazing," she gasped, lost in the feeling of both of them around and inside of her.

And then she came, hard and sudden, body overloaded from the myriad of sensations. Just as she was starting to come back down, Aidan trembled beneath her and Virgil tensed behind her, and she went over again with them.

They lay there for what seemed like forever. It had been one of the most intense experiences of her life.

She whimpered in protest as Virgil rolled off of her and shortly after deprived her of Aidan as he pulled her down between them. After the initial loss, the buzz returned. God, but she felt good. Decadent beyond belief.

"Wow," she said finally.

"Told you." Virgil was smug beside her.

"Liked it then?" Aidan was less smug and more, well, Aidan. Always thinking about someone else before himself.

"Yeah, I did. I really did." She stretched luxuriously between them, feeling her muscles protest. She had a notion she'd be paying the price of that for a few days. But, oh, was it worth it.

Chapter Twenty-two

Predictably, Raymond Craig was in his office when Virgil returned home that afternoon.

He didn't bother knocking, which earned him an amused smirk instead of a reprimand before his uncle turned back to the work before him.

"A bit of friendly advice, Virgil," Raymond said, his tone casual and smooth, almost affable. "While you can't prevent all gossip, the three of you might want to be a trifle more discreet in the future."

Virgil felt his blood rise. "And what exactly are you implying?"

Raymond shuffled the papers before him and set them aside. "Only that you should be more considerate of Drea's reputation in the community. Leaving your bike parked out in the open behind the store last night and well into this morning is going to start tongues wagging." He then removed his glasses and turned his full attention to Virgil. "Especially when it's the second evening in a row."

"We've been friends since way back, Uncle. Everyone in Morton's Pointe knows that." Virgil tried to keep his voice even.

"Perhaps. Though things are perceived differently when you're twenty-three than when you were thirteen. There are no innocent sleepovers at your age."

He hated it when his uncle made a good point.

"Add in the fact that the store didn't open until almost eleven this morning..." There was a speculative spark in the steel eyes. "Drea may run the sole general store in town, but she still needs to maintain a somewhat irreproachable appearance in the community's eye. They respected her father and have grown to respect her, but they'll have no qualms about heading to Boyne City or Charlevoix for supplies if her morals become questionable. You can never be too careful with small-town minds."

"They're not that narrow minded," Virgil retorted, though he knew full well that his uncle was dead on the money.

Raymond snorted derisively. "When you flaunt something in their faces they are. There's more going on behind the closed doors in this town than you can begin to dream of, son. But that's where it stays, behind closed doors, if only figuratively speaking. There really aren't many secrets in places the size of Morton's Pointe. But as long as people can pretend they don't know what's going on, things are fine. Wave it in their faces and you'll pay dearly."

Virgil worked his jaw. It was difficult to argue when he made such valid points. Especially when they were things that *should* have occurred to Virgil but had not once crossed his mind. But his priority had been making sure he didn't lose Drea or Aidan. He hadn't given any thought beyond seeing whether or not the three of them could have a physical relationship together. Maybe he'd hoped that everything else would sort itself out if that worked.

"You're young, Virgil." Raymond stood and walked around the desk, stopping a foot or so away. "Consequences don't really factor into your thinking yet. You haven't seen enough to have learned that lesson. You will, eventually."

"So why not let me learn it, then? You're about fourteen years too late to start playing my father, Uncle," Virgil spat.

There was no trace of emotion on Raymond's face or in his voice when he said evenly, "Yes, I've been such an ogre all these years, making certain you've wanted for nothing and *not* packing you off to boarding school at the first opportunity. How miserable you must have been." His lips curled in amusement. "If you're going to argue with me, Virgil, try to make certain the point you are arguing actually has something to back it up."

A number of comments rose to mind, but Virgil quickly discarded them all. Raymond would more than likely laugh them off or turn them against Virgil. If only he weren't so damned unflappable. Raymond could get as riled as Virgil, but one didn't achieve the success Raymond had in life by losing his cool every time he was challenged.

"Giving up so soon? I thought you'd at least want to take me to task for nearly bedding your girl." Raymond sighed as if Virgil had disappointed him greatly with the omission. The amused glint in his eyes belied any truth to the feeling.

Virgil felt the urge to hit his uncle rise again but held back. While hitting him would be satisfying, it wouldn't solve anything. But the comment couldn't go unanswered. "If you go after her again, Uncle, I will take you down."

That earned him a genuine smile. "No threats of physical violence, but something more lasting. I'm impressed, Virgil."

"Stay away from her," Virgil hissed.

"Seeing as Morton's Pointe is as small as it is, with only my one bank and her one general store, staying away is impossible. I also enjoy Drea's company. So if the opportunity arises again, I won't avoid it." Then the cool, businesslike demeanor dropped and Virgil was left facing Raymond Craig the man, not the entrepreneur. "But seeing as I'm full of advice this afternoon, let me give you one more piece, Virgil. If you and that Morrison boy can manage to keep her needs satisfied, you won't need to worry about me. But rest assured, I will take *full* advantage of any opportunity presented to me."

Virgil opened his mouth to protest but Raymond held up his hand.

"This discussion is over, Virgil. Now go and wash up. Oswald will have dinner on shortly."

Ↄ

After a very long night with little sleep, Virgil rode into town early the next morning. He hadn't stopped thinking about what his uncle had said. The three of them needed to figure out how they were going to handle things in public. They could stick with the outward appearance of friendship, but going that route left them open to pursuit from other parties. And you could only turn people down so many times before everyone got suspicious.

Then there was the issue of Uncle Raymond. Virgil needed to get Aidan alone to discuss that. The chances of ever convincing Drea the man was up to no good with regards to her were slim to none. He and Aidan had to figure out how to keep Raymond from being a threat without pissing Drea off in the process.

Parking his bike behind the store, Virgil headed in through the back door. He noted with amusement the perfectly fitted piece of plywood replacing the pane of glass Aidan had broken the other night. If Aidan had access to glass, he would have tried fixing it proper. It surprised Virgil that Aidan hadn't painted the wood white to match the door. Or maybe he hadn't gotten around to it yet.

"Drea, stop it," he heard Aidan's voice demand from the front of the store. "Someone could walk in."

Drea wasn't put off. "Remember that annoying little door chime that rings every time someone comes in? It makes for a nice warning, and we're well out of sight. Besides, no one hardly ever shows up before noon in the winter."

Any further protests of Aidan's were muffled. Virgil discovered just why when he saw that Aidan had himself an armful of Drea, who was doing her damnedest to keep him from talking.

They were well concealed from the main entrance by the canned goods shelves, but it wasn't perfect. If they got too caught up and didn't hear the bell...Virgil really hated his uncle.

"People don't always use the front door," he announced loud enough to startle them apart.

Aidan looked embarrassed. Drea shrugged it off after the initial surprise passed.

"Get up on the wrong side of the bed?" She straightened her dress.

Seeing as he'd hardly slept, there hadn't been much getting up for it to go wrong or right. "I'm saying that you can't rely on that bell to keep you from being caught in a compromising situation."

Her eyes narrowed. "I thought you'd be the last to disapprove. Unless maybe you're not as fine with things as you claim to be."

Aidan's hand rested gently on her shoulder. "Virgil's right and you know it. Don't go picking a fight with him for nothing."

Virgil was tempted to say something about Aidan taking his side again in so many days but decided goading Drea into a temper really wasn't in their best interests.

"Fine," she grumbled. "So what's got you in such a bad mood? You and Raymond didn't get into it again, did you?"

He really wished she wouldn't say his uncle's name like he was a good friend. But that was a battle for another day. "No." He managed to sound normal. "My uncle and I had a rather calm discussion, and it made me aware of some things I should have realized sooner. Things we all should have realized."

That drew a concerned look from Aidan. "What's going on, Virgil?"

Virgil walked down to the main floor to join them, leaning back against the counter when he reached them. "While we may have gotten our situation straightened out between the three of us, there's a few details we have to figure out."

"Such as?" Drea wondered.

"First off, we need to decide whether or not our relationship is going to change publicly," Virgil stated. "We can't rightly announce to everyone that the three of us are fooling around together."

"Why announce anything?" She still didn't seem to get it.

Aidan, however, did. "Because people such as Bill Wellington will think you're available, Drea."

She groaned. "Are either of you ever going to forget about that? Bill's clueless. I could be married, and he'd continue to chase after me. It's a fact of life." She threw her hands up in disgust, the light catching on Great-Gran Morrison's ring resting comfortably on her right hand.

It gave Virgil an idea. "People must have started to speculate, what with Aidan working here all the time, don't you think? Friends grow closer, relationships change."

"What are you going on about?" Drea's brows drew together

in confusion.

"Remember back when Aidan gave you the ring, how pissed I was? And how I was none too happy to see you actually wearing it when I got back? I can't have been the only person thinking like that," he pressed.

"Now you're saying you want Aidan and I to get hitched so people stay off our backs?"

"Not that far, but giving the outward appearance of being engaged wouldn't hurt none," he corrected.

"You really are quite pragmatic when you put your mind to it, Virgil."

"You don't think it's crazy, then?" Virgil asked him.

"Something's not crazy when it makes sense."

"Hold on a minute," Drea protested. "No offense, Aidan, but I have no interest in getting married. To either of you. And a marriage would be expected eventually if there's a betrothal."

Aidan turned her to face him. "Drea, it'd buy us some time to figure our situation out without other people getting in the mix."

Drea glanced back at Virgil. "How's that fair to you if it looks like I'm engaged to him? Aren't people going to wonder why you aren't looking for someone?"

He shrugged. "It's easier on men. Everyone will probably think I'm following in Uncle Raymond's footsteps and taking my pleasure elsewhere."

Drea frowned in thought. "Aidan works at the store with me, and now that we're supposedly engaged, that explains why he's here a lot. But won't people still wonder why you're over all the time?"

"Good friends always visit," he replied as if the answer was obvious.

But even Aidan seemed concerned. "Drea's got a point. It would make more sense for you to be engaged to her. Then we'd both have reasons for being around so often."

Virgil shook his head. "No, the engagement between you two makes more sense. It won't take much convincing people as it's what they think already."

"I should have started looking into work elsewhere a while ago," Aidan said. "You can take my place here."

"Raymond wants him at the bank," Drea chimed in. "Right?"

"Unfortunately," Virgil sighed.

"So the whole fake engagement really wouldn't solve anything," Drea pointed out.

No, it wouldn't.

"I wish there was more to do around here. Then I *could* justify both of you being here to help out. Although..." she trailed off in thought. "I have been wanting to put some money from the homestead to use businesswise, an expansion to the store or new venture altogether."

"Like what, a soda shop?" Aidan offered, attempting to get where she was going. It was more than Virgil was capable of at the moment.

"Soda shops are great, but really not that big of a draw, except with the tourists in the summer. Besides, this town already has one up at Birch's drugstore."

"What else is there?" Virgil asked. "Not much really goes well with a general store."

"Well, there is something," she said. "You have to promise not to get pissed, Virgil, all right?"

Getting pissed could mean it likely involved one person. He sighed. "I promise."

Taking a deep breath, she forged ahead. "I've been bouncing a few ideas off Raymond, because if anyone would know what would work or not, he would. And he was telling me about the business boom that happened when the state enacted prohibition. Even though it's looking likely that it will be repealed here in Michigan, it's probably going to pass as a constitutional amendment to be enforced nationally."

"What's that have to do with us here?" Aidan asked.

"If it does go national, then people are going to be needing to get their alcohol somewhere. Raymond was telling me how businesses downstate were used as fronts for liquor clubs run out of their basements or backrooms."

"Drea, that's illegal. You don't want to be doing something that brings you head-to-head with the law." Virgil grabbed her arm to get her attention.

"But it won't. It was barely ever enforced when it was a state law, why would it be any better nationally? And it's not like there's much notice taken of a little town in the middle of nowhere." She beamed up at him. "You know the people of this town; they like their drink and found ways to get it when they weren't supposed to."

Raymond's words about the many secrets of the town's inhabitants came back to Virgil. "It's a big risk, Drea, especially as an excuse for the three of us to spend more time together. There has to be another option."

"But not half so fun or profitable," she countered.

Further argument was stalled by the chiming of the front door. She darted off to take care of her customer before they could protest.

"It's insane," Virgil said to Aidan. "And there's no guarantee that prohibition is going to pass."

"No guarantee, but very likely."

Virgil realized that Aidan wasn't arguing like he'd expected. "You think it's a good idea?"

"It's dangerous as hell, but it might be worth trying." He held up a hand to stay any comment Virgil intended to make. "It's too soon for you to experience it yet, but things around here are too normal after where we've been. I'm not saying I'm bored or hate it here, only that it would be nice to have something to mix things up a bit."

"You're supposed to be the voice of reason," Virgil protested.

"And you're supposed to be all for the crazy ideas." Aidan smirked.

"I don't think it's wise."

"Because it comes from Raymond, right?"

A very large part was because of that. But if the suggestion had come from Raymond, it meant the man saw it as an acceptable risk venture; he was first and foremost a businessman. If his uncle thought it worth considering, maybe it was.

"Humor Drea for now," Aidan suggested. "We'll see if prohibition even goes through. In the meantime, we can probably come up with alternatives. You were the one who started all this."

"I did," Virgil admitted.

The bell over the front door jangled again, and Drea rejoined.

"Of course, the one time I actually *want* Gladys North to come in the store," Aidan teased.

Drea swatted him. "Looks like the two of you are going to have to tell me I'm crazy to my face then."

"You're not crazy, Drea," Virgil grudged. "The criminal

element aside, do you even have the first idea about running a liquor business?"

"Business is business, Virgil," she said, as if it should be obvious to anyone with half a brain. "It all pretty much comes down to keeping the customer happy by either giving them what they want or making them think they want what you have."

Great, she was starting to think like his uncle. Maybe Drea's old man wasn't so stupid for attempting to keep Drea out of the business end of the store. She had a sharp mind. It was strange seeing her so pragmatic, although there was no denying she really did seem to know what she was about. It occurred to him that his uncle's attraction to Drea wasn't purely sexual, that her interest in business attracted him as well. Great, he didn't need to throw jealousy over that into the mix, too. Or maybe he did. It would definitely guarantee that he never let his guard down concerning his uncle. Raymond had warned Virgil that he would take full advantage of any opportunity left open to him.

Virgil reached for Drea and tugged her close. "I really think I came home at the right time."

Her brow furrowed in confusion. "Why's that?"

"Because there's only room in the world for one Raymond Craig."

Drea's mouth opened to protest.

Aidan spoke up before she could. "Virgil's got a point."

"Excuse me?" She whirled on him, turning her back on Virgil. Which Virgil took full advantage of as he moved up and wrapped himself around her. "Hey!" she protested.

He chuckled as he leaned down to murmur in her ear, "Now there's the Drea Samuels I remember. Level-headed is all well and fine, but I like the fire better."

Aidan shook his head bemusedly.

Drea called him on it. "What's so funny, Aidan?"

"The more things change, the more they stay the same." He stepped forward and gently cupped her face. "You and Virgil may be getting better at thinking things through before acting, but it still takes nothing to get you riled."

"And Aidan's never going to be able to keep from stepping in and making sure you and I don't kill each other," Virgil added with a wink to Aidan.

"I wouldn't be so sure about that. I've found I enjoy getting involved." He leaned around Drea and captured Virgil's mouth in a quick, hungry kiss before pulling back. "Sometimes it's more fun adding fuel to the fire than trying to put it out."

The bell over the door chimed again, announcing another customer. Drea automatically started away, but Virgil held her in place.

"We're not done yet," he stated. Then to Aidan, "You mind seeing to that?"

"If it's Gladys, you owe me." He headed to the front of the store.

"For someone who was all worried about people catching us in compromising positions, you're running a pretty big risk of that," Drea hissed at Virgil, but the words lacked any serious venom. He could tell she was pretending to be more upset than she was.

"Some things are worth the risk."

"What, like holding me hostage here until I give up on the crazy notion of the speakeasy?"

"No."

"Promise to stop seeing Raymond?"

If only. "I know I stand a better chance of seeing hell freeze over."

She laughed at that. "So what, then?"

He caught Gladys North's voice from the front of the store. "Oh, Aidan, I was hoping you'd attend to me today. Annabelle did the most fascinating thing last night."

Drea stifled a giggle. "Aidan's going to kill you, you know."

"I have no doubt." He grinned. "And I finally figured out exactly what I'm going to do with you."

"And?"

He lifted her up and walked farther into the back of the store.

"Virgil?"

"I have a feeling Aidan's going to be awhile. And I've decided"—he caught the lobe of her ear lightly in his teeth, delighting in her quiet gasp—"that I'd like to be convinced that you can fool around in the store without letting the customers know."

She craned her neck to smirk up at him. "Or maybe you realized you were jealous when you caught us, so you're getting some of your own back now."

"You could be right." He kissed Drea then, losing himself in her until Aidan could show up and catch them. There were more enjoyable things to be doing instead of worrying about the future.

About the Author

Emery Sanborne considers herself a work in progress. She loves Philadelphia, Lake Michigan, taking long walks through old cemeteries, accents from the British Isles and writing. While she has yet to fall in love, she holds onto the hope of one day being completely swept off her feet by something other than a really good book or the strong city wind.

To learn more about Emery Sanborne and her other works, please visit www.emerysanborne.com. She can be reached at emery_sanborne@yahoo.com.

*Duty wars with affection when Racor's greatest spy must decide
who to trust, the evidence against her sexy suspects,
or her heart?*

A Scorching Seduction
© 2007 Marie Harte

Lt. Col. Trace N'Tre and Assassin Vaan C'Vail are hiding
out in the only place the military can't touch them—on a
pleasure planet in an island resort owned by Vaan's cousin.
Gathering evidence on the outside, they know it's only a matter
of time before they'll have to face their accuser, a high official in
the Racor government.

Unbeknownst to them, Myst, Racor's greatest spy, has had
her eyes on them for some time. The puzzle of these two alleged
traitors doesn't fit, and Myst has made it her mission to find out
why. But when the tables are turned and she's caught spying
under the planet's hot summer suns, pleasure and affection
confuse the issue, making her wonder who to trust—her heart,
or the evidence against her lovers.

Warning, this title contains the following: explicit sex, frank
language, ménage, m/m action, and hot sweaty adventure.

Available now in ebook from Samhain Publishing.

Enjoy the following excerpt from A Scorching Seduction...

Trace stared at her from head to toe as they left the gymnasium for the hallway. "Where are you from, Fia?"

"Nowhere, really. I was orphaned when I was three and grew up shuttled between Jergin and Aptor. That's where most foundlings are raised." She noted the softening in Trace's, if not Vaan's, face. Vaan, the assassin, remained wary. Yet Trace, Racor's legendary assault commander, was a sucker for a woman with a sob story. "I had a very loving childhood, though. And when I reached my majority at fifteen, I decided to become a sex sharer. It's respectable work and pays very well."

Vaan lifted a brow at Trace, who scowled but said nothing.

"That's what I've always told my friend here. Sex is to be treasured, explored, not deemed dirty or wrong." Vaan stared smugly at Trace.

Fia frowned, enjoying her role. "But if you feel that way, Trace, then why are you here?"

"Good question," he muttered, and Vaan chuckled.

"Don't mind Trace. He's just upset that I got the better of him in our entanglement."

"Shut up, Vaan." Trace's gaze narrowed, and Fia encouraged his small temper, knowing it would aid her as a distraction.

"But you both seemed so wrapped in each other," she said earnestly. "Trace, your climax was so beautiful, Vaan's hands so giving." To her delight, Trace flushed and Vaan grinned widely.

"I told you I knew what you needed," Vaan murmured.

"And I told you I'd make you pay for that." Trace kept Fia

between them while his attention fixated on Vaan.

"Um, I hate to interrupt," Fia said meekly. "But would it be okay if I cleaned up in my chambers before we met Vela?" She blushed, staring at her bare feet. "I want to maintain a good impression, and I feel a trifle, ah, used."

Vaan glanced from Trace to her, his eyes gleaming. "I don't think I've ever seen you look better, Fia. You're practically glowing." Damn. Now Trace looked speculative as he stared at her. "But all right. Take us to your room."

Within minutes, they stood in her spartan quarters. Unlike Clea's side of the room, Fia's had little adornment. Only a silken bedsheet and a blooming orvid marked the room as hers. While they checked the security of her windowless room, she worked on appearing shy, demure. A difficult task with a bed so near the objects of her desire. "Um, I don't suppose you'd let me change in private?" She forced another blush. "I'm not used to dressing in front of others."

Vaan's eyebrows rose. "What? You're just used to undressing in front of others? You are a sex sharer, aren't you?"

She called on some tears and forced a flush.

Trace shot Vaan a sharp look and the light-haired assassin sighed. "We'll be right outside, Fia. And don't even think about running away or there'll be hell to pay." His eyes burned as they lingered over her breasts.

The minute they left, she jammed the security box by the door, buying her a little time.

She'd been more than pleased to share Clea's room, partial to the hidden chamber directly behind the armoire, a secret meeting place Clea and Vela liked to use when Vela felt naughty.

Moving with a sense of urgency, Fia threw a few sets of clothing and a pair of sandals, her communicator—which didn't work except in one small area deeper into the island—a knife and a map into a small bag and passed into Clea's secret chamber. From there, she squeezed through a narrow window leading to the central garden and inner courtyard. She quickly weaved through guests and curious staff alike, nodding pleasantly while gauging how much distance she'd put between herself and the men trained to hunt down their prey until found.

She could only hope she'd given herself enough time.

Welcome to Fantasm Island! Leave your inhibitions at the door and let your fantasies soar.

Fantasmagorical
© *2007 Annmarie McKenna*

That's what the brochure said anyway. A week long fling with a stranger. Where's the harm in that? Take a compatibility quiz and a slew of other health tests, sign a strict privacy agreement and give license to any sexual fantasy you've ever had. Evan Knight couldn't wait.

Gabe and Lance have been searching for their perfect third for what seems like forever. One look at the woman he and his best friend and lover Lance have chosen to claim during her time on the island, and Gabe thinks they may have finally found her.

But what if Evan isn't interested in more than the fling she signed up for? Or worse, what if she can't handle two men who are into each other too? Gabe and Lance have one week to convince Evan that the three of them belong together...and they'll use every bit of seduction in their arsenal to make sure when the fantasy ends, their reality together will only just be beginning.

Warning, this title contains the following: explicit fantasmagorical sex, graphic language, ménage a trois, and hot nekkid man-love.

Available now in ebook from Samhain Publishing.

Printed in the United Kingdom
by Lightning Source UK Ltd.
132738UK00001B/231/P